I0788233

The Heart of the Dawn

THE SONG THAT STAYS
Volume I

The Heart of the Dawn

By Joseph Moro

Published by Joseph Moro
Cover and interior design by Joseph Moro

First Edition

For Cheri —

Whose love I never deserved,

Who searched for me even when I ran,

And whom I will love beyond the boundaries of time

itself.

May the world see her now as I have always seen her

—

The mercy that never turned away.

Thank you, Janis and Florence, for the beta reading and insight.

To Adrienne, who never stops telling the world I am a 'famous author,' and whose belief in my success runs deeper than I can repay. May this book sell so well that I can one day fund the dreams she carries—college, and all the tomorrows beyond.

And For Mel — Who thinks she deserves this.

"What the world fears, light remembers with mercy."

— Dawnkeeper Saying

THE HEART OF THE DAWN — CONTENTS

Prologue — The First Light

Chapter One — The Dream and the Doubt

Chapter Two — The Lesson of Suffering

Chapter Three — The Weight of Obedience

Chapter Four — The River Between

Chapter Five — Faith in Motion

Chapter Six — The Rust and the Ravens

Chapter Seven — Dreams of Ash and Light

Chapter Eight — The Innocent and the Heretic

Chapter Nine — The Test of Mercy

Chapter Ten — The Road Between

Chapter Eleven — Faithheart's Return

Chapter Twelve — Echoes of Dawnfire

Chapter Thirteen — Where Mercy Meets

Chapter Fourteen — Building a Home

Chapter Fifteen — Festival of Light

Chapter Sixteen — The Unfinished Wedding

Chapter Seventeen — The Circle of Dawn

Chapter Eighteen — The Voice in the Light

Prologue — The First Light

♥ ✳ ♥ ✳ ♥

The Burning Hall

She was not yet silver-haired when Tess Belanna crossed the border into a land that worshiped certainty more than wonder. In her homeland, prayer lived in breath and river-song, and magic healed like morning mending the horizon. Her order did not bind power—it learned its shape.

But a whisper stirred in her bones like sunrise behind closed eyes:

Go north.

A child of the dawn wakes in chains.

So she obeyed.

She crossed sea and frost-struck roads, starlight caught in her hair her only banner. But the further she walked, the dimmer that thread became—as though the world itself tried to swallow where she came from, and why.

This land had forgotten gentle power; faith had hardened into law, healing into hierarchy.

No birds greeted her at the gates of Stoneward Reach—only wary eyes, hollow and clinging to order like a drowning hand to stone.

Tess did not stop. Approval had never been her compass. She had come for him. Her task was not to guide his future, only to keep his light alive long enough for the world to recognize it.

Smoke reached her first—then the crackle of beams collapsing, the screams, the fists against barred wood.

Tess ran. Branches tore her hem; ash stung her lungs. The world blurred into heat and fear—until she saw it:

A refuge hall burning. Mothers clawed at doors while priests shouted prayers instead of breaking locks.

She dove through fire.

Flame roared, shoving breath from her chest—and then the air changed.

Not hers.

His.

A boy stood in the inferno, shaking with terror and purpose. Soot streaked his cheeks; tears cut clean paths through the ash. From his small trembling body poured power so pure it bent fire aside like wheat in the wind.

Flames did not consume him; they curved around the children in sheltering light. Smoke stilled. Heat recoiled. It was not destruction. It was dawn—raw and instinctive—protecting life.

Tess fell to her knees.

This was no wild force.

This was mercy given form.

He wasn't born to break, but to mend.

When the rafters collapsed and light faded, he crumpled—not from power unleashed, but from the weight of a world too afraid to understand him.

She reached for him—

—but hands seized her first.

"Devourer!"

Maldrin strode forward, gold-threaded robes gleaming, his face a mask of sorrowing pride. Villagers shrank beneath his words as if guilt were gravity.

"He unleashed ruin. Bind him—before chaos spreads."

Fear swallowed reason whole.

Tess strained against the arms that held her. He saved them. You saw.

But fear is loud, and truth seldom wins the first hearing.

Maldrin pressed a burning sigil to the child's chest.

The boy writhed—not from flame, but from shame forced where wonder lived. Tess felt something sacred tear apart in her chest.

A silver thread fell from her hair.

The boy collapsed, light smothered beneath chains engraved with righteousness.

"Order is restored," Maldrin declared.

Praise rose like smoke.

Lies always rise fastest.

The Vow and the Cost

Night came. Guards slept.

Tess slipped through shadow and knelt beside the boy where he lay hidden in a cold dormitory cell. His face was peaceful—the false peace of a spirit drugged by fear.

"You are not danger," she whispered.

"You are dawn."

Her hand hovered above the burning seal.

Her vow pulsed in her bones.

She touched the mark.

It shuddered.

A thread loosened.

A strand of starlight left her hair.

This was not mercy as the Temple preached it—
this was mercy as the dawn understood it, ancient and
alive.

The boy stirred—and forgot her.

Tess exhaled through breaking rib and spirit.

She would weaken it again.

And again.

Until light remembered itself.

Even if every touch made him forget her all over again.

Even if her hair silvered like frost.

Even if he grew never knowing her name.

This was not martyrdom.

It was faith in what love could become.

The Years of Silvering

In the deep woods she built a refuge woven of branch and river-hum. Seasons passed; silver threads gathered in her lap like fallen moons.

Sometimes she woke gasping—fire behind her lids, not terror but glory rejected.

Other nights she dreamed of him older—gentle hands, solemn eyes, never using power to take, only to mend. Beside him, a woman warm as sunrise.

Not a warrior.

A healer.

A heart that would teach him what she could not
stay to teach:

Power cannot be controlled into goodness.

It must be trusted into truth.

Years unfolded.

The boy grew.

He learned obedience but lived compassion. He
carried buckets for those who mocked him. He
touched wounded seedlings as though they were
sacred. He looked at the world not as threat, but as
something aching to be healed.

Sometimes he paused, brows knit, as half-
remembered words surfaced like stones in a river:

Mercy is older than fear.

Light need not prove itself to be true.

Love endures what control cannot hold.

Each time, the hidden scar flickered—and Tess felt another strand fall from her hair.

She did not mourn what she lost.

Only what he bore.

Destiny gathers quietly before it breaks like thunder.

One day the scar on his chest would burn awake, and the temple that called him danger would fall.

That would not be her day.

Her task was not to stand beside him at triumph, only to keep the door cracked until he could walk through it unafraid.

Still, she smiled beneath the trees as sunrise spilled like blessing through needles.

Light, once awakened, never sleeps—and love will find him not as myth, but as flesh and breath.

Tess looked toward the east.

"Rise, Heart of the Dawn," she whispered to the wind.

"And remember yourself."

Far across the same world, in a cottage that leaned tiredly against the wind,

a little girl jolted awake.

Cheri sat upright beneath her patched blanket, breath shaking, heart racing.

The dream clung to her like smoke.

A hall on fire.

Children crying.

And a small boy standing in the blaze—scared, shaken, but shining like dawn breaking through a storm.

The flames bent around him instead of devouring him.

He had looked nothing like a monster.

Cheri wiped her eyes with the heel of her hand just as footsteps thudded down the hall.

Her mother shoved open the door with a sigh heavy enough to bend the frame.

"What now?" she muttered. "Crying over dreams again?"

Cheri swallowed. "Mama… there was a boy in the fire. He saved—"

"Oh, nonsense." Her mother waved her off. "Dreams are just noise in your head, child. Stupid things. Worthless things."

Another sigh, sharper this time. "If you're going to wake the whole house, at least dream about something useful."

Cheri's throat tightened. "But it felt real."

"Everything feels real to children."

Her mother pinched the bridge of her nose. "Go back to sleep. And stop filling your head with foolish stories."

She closed the door before Cheri could reply.

Left in the quiet, Cheri curled beneath the blanket, hugging her knees, the dream still burning bright behind her closed eyes.

She didn't understand the boy in the fire.

She didn't understand why her mother's voice hurt more than the dream.

But she knew one thing:

He hadn't been dangerous.

He had been merciful.

And he had been alone.

She whispered into the dark, as if someone might hear,

"I believe you."

Cheri never dreamed of the boy again.

Not for ten years.

Chapter One — The Dream and the Doubt

"Doubt may guard the door, but only faith dares knock."

♥ ✳ ♥ ✳ ♥

The Dream and the Doubt

Cheri woke before the sun. For a long moment she lay still beneath the woven blanket, the echo of the dream holding her like a tide that refused to recede. Her heart beat fast—not from fear, but from a certainty she couldn't name.

A man stood amid light and ash, eyes like sunrise after a storm, and a voice—clear as bells over water—whispered, He isn't the Destroyer. He's the Heart of the Dawn.

She whispered the words aloud, testing their weight in the waking air. They felt strange on her tongue—both sacred and forbidden.

A chill breeze slipped through the shutter gap. Beyond the cottage walls, the village still slept; the hearth's last ember glowed faintly. The quiet felt heavy enough to hold meaning.

Cheri rose, wrapped a shawl around her shoulders, and crossed to the window. Frost veiled the glass in silver lace. She drew a small circle in the fog and peered through it. The world outside looked thin, pale—half dream itself. She had always felt the world more deeply than she knew how to explain, and it often left her standing between certainty and faith with no map for either.

Somewhere north, beyond the hills, she felt the pull again.
Not direction—summons.

She pressed her palm over her heartbeat and breathed out slowly. "Faith first, logic second", Janis always said. But faith in what exactly? A vision? A whisper?

♥ ✳ ♥ ✳ ♥

Hearthlight Warnings

The latch creaked.

"You're up early," Patty murmured, her voice still wrapped in sleep. She rubbed her eyes and shuffled sink, pouring water into the kettle and setting it on the stove without looking.

"I couldn't rest."

"Another dream?"

"Not another—the same."

Patty frowned. "The one with the fire?"

Cheri nodded.

"The one where you hear voices?"

"Only one," Cheri said. "It doesn't frighten me."

"Cheri, you said it told you the Destroyer was—"

"Not the Destroyer," Cheri said softly. "The Heart of the Dawn."

Patty sighed "You know what people call blasphemy around here. You'll start a sermon you can't finish."

"It wasn't blasphemy," Cheri said. "It was truth."

"You think truth comes through dreams?"

"I think it comes however the dawn decides."

The kettle began its slow whisper. Warmth spread through the tiny kitchen, scented with herbs and ash.

Patty leaned against the table, arms crossed. "You've always been like this—hear a story, make it prophecy."

Cheri smiled, but privately she wished someone would understand how her heart carried meaning the way other people carried memory.

Cheri laughed, soft and clean as wind through chimes. "And when the world didn't end, I gave the candles to the chapel."

"That's not the point."

"I think it is," Cheri said gently. "I'd rather prepare light than expect darkness."

Patty looked away, jaw tight, voice softening. "You've a good heart. I just don't want to see it broken chasing shadows."

Rumors in the Market

Cheri turned back to the window. The frost had melted enough for her to see the ridge of hills catching first light—a faint gold line along the horizon.

"Maybe shadows are where light begins," she whispered.

Patty rolled her eyes, affection in it. "Philosopher at sunrise. Saints preserve me."

Cheri smiled. "Maybe they already do."

The kettle whistled. They moved with the rhythm of long friendship—one grounding, the other dreaming.

When they sat, Patty drummed her fingers. "You're thinking of going north again, aren't you?"

Cheri's hand stilled on her cup.

"I can always tell."

"I don't know why," Cheri admitted. "Only that something waits there."

"You and your destiny talk."

"Maybe destiny is just love that hasn't found its place yet."

Patty stared for a long moment, then looked down. "Promise me—if you go, come back with proof. Don't bring home another dream."

Cheri reached across the table, squeezed her hand. "If I find what I'm meant to, you'll see proof enough."

Outside, the first rays of morning climbed the hills like slow-burning fire. Cheri rose, wrapping her shawl tighter, and stood by the door. For a moment, she could almost hear music in the wind—faint, distant, like someone humming far away in the forest.

She closed her eyes and whispered a prayer she didn't entirely understand.
Show me the Heart of the Dawn.

By midmorning, smoke rose from hearths and carts creaked along the muddy road. Cheri's shawl caught the light as she walked toward the market square, basket in hand, her head still full of the dream.

The vendors greeted her kindly—but warmth in a small town could shift faster than weather. She felt eyes linger. Conversations stopped mid-sentence.

At the baker's stall, old Mira leaned forward. "You heard, child? The temple down south—burned again. They say the Devourer's curse spread through their ranks."

Cheri's fingers tightened around her coin. "A curse?"

"Aye. My cousin's boy's a novice there. Says one of their own turned against them. Fire from within the walls this time, not lightning. They say it's a sign the Destroyer walks again."

The word snagged against Cheri's ribs. "They said the same years ago. Maybe it's still just men who start fires, not monsters."

Mira frowned. "Careful talk, love. Doubt their tales and they'll brand you with it."

"I'm not doubting," Cheri said softly. "I'm remembering who saved the children the first time."

Mira only crossed herself and handed over the bread. "Best not speak of such mercy. People don't like when kindness interferes with punishment."

She moved from stall to stall—herbs, apples, cloth—collecting whispers as easily as supplies. Each retelling of the Devourer's story grew darker, like a shadow stretching with the day.

Counsel of Janis and Michael

By the river path, her chest ached with the weight of other people's fear.

Winter had not quite left; ice still clung to shaded roots, and the current hummed low. She stopped beneath an alder tree, her eyes following the shimmer of the water.

Her parents had loved rivers too—not for beauty, but for escape. Each time a preacher's words clashed with theirs, they packed the wagon and followed the next current. Truth must match the heart, her father said, or the heart must move on.
But his truth changed with the wind. Her mother's temper changed faster.

Faith became something Cheri learned to hold alone—not in walls, not in books, but in the quiet between breaths.

A breeze stirred. The surface caught the sun and flared white-gold for an instant—light rising from water. Her pulse quickened.

He isn't the Destroyer. He's the Heart of the Dawn.

"Pretty sight, isn't it?"

Cheri turned. Janis led her mare down the path, reins loose, breath fogging in the chill. Her smile made people talk softer without knowing why.

"You're up early," Janis said. "Patty said you were haunting the market before the bell even rang."

"I couldn't sleep."

"Dream again?"

Cheri nodded.

Janis dismounted, walking beside her. "Dreams are messengers, not maps," she said at last. "They tell us which way to turn our hearts, not which road to walk."

"That's the problem," Cheri murmured. "My heart keeps pointing north, and my feet don't know if it's faith or folly."

Janis chuckled softly. "You think I knew the difference when Michael asked me to follow him into a storm to start our homestead? Half of faith is pretending you already have it."

"Patty says pretending leads to disappointment."

"Patty would call rain untrustworthy because it falls too much like tears."

That earned a small laugh, and Janis's eyes warmed.

They walked until Janis's cottage came into view— stone walls under ivy, smoke curling from the chimney. Michael was stacking logs by the door, humming some wordless tune.

"Stay for tea," Janis said. "Michael thinks we're out of leaves, but that's just his excuse to see people."

Inside, warmth wrapped Cheri like an embrace. The scent of cedar and mint filled the room. Michael grinned as she entered. "Back from saving the world yet, Cheri?"

"Not today," she said.

"Well, save it slowly then. Gives the rest of us time to catch up."

Janis swatted him with a towel. "Don't tease her for listening to her heart."

"Listening, sure. Following—different story."

He winked, but the look he shared with Janis carried the peace of people who had built their faith in storms.

Over tea, talk turned to the temple rumors. Michael's expression sobered. "Be careful with those dreams, Cheri. People need their monsters. They don't like hearing they might be wrong about them."

Janis touched Cheri's hand. "Still—sometimes mercy hides in the monster. Remember that."

Cheri looked between them, warmth rising behind her ribs. "You believe me, then?"

"I believe the heart recognizes what the world forgets," Janis said. "If the dawn is whispering, listen."

Michael nodded reluctantly. "Just don't expect everyone else to hear the same tune."

"Maybe they don't need to," Cheri said. "Maybe I just need to follow it."

The River Sign

When she left, afternoon softened toward gold. She walked slow, the river on her left, Janis's words echoing like a gentle whisper: Dreams are messengers, not maps.

But her dream burned brighter than any message she'd ever been given. Somewhere in the northern hills, something waited—not a monster, not a curse, but a promise.

Evening laid gold over the water before surrendering to blue. The river hummed low, steady, like a heartbeat beneath the world. Cheri stood at its edge, cold brushing her boots.

He isn't the Destroyer. He's the Heart of the Dawn.

The voice from her dream echoed in the running water. She looked north, to the ridges dissolving into mist—peace there, and promise—but she didn't yet understand either.

She cupped her hands in the stream. The chill bit, anchoring her. "If this is truly from You," she whispered, "show me the path. Make the light unmistakable."

For a heartbeat, nothing. Then the water caught the last of the sunset and shone white-gold, bright enough to sting her eyes.

It wasn't fire or reflection. It was reminder.

A hush so complete she could hear her own heart answering.

Cheri swallowed. "Then I'll follow—when You call again."

She walked home slowly through twilight fields. The cottage lamps glowed ahead like a single star. When she opened the door, the scent of tea and smoke met her like comfort.

Patty sat by the hearth mending a curtain. "You were gone a long time."

"I needed to think."

"Dangerous habit."

"Maybe. But I think I know what I need to do."

Patty's needle paused. "Please tell me it doesn't involve chasing omens into the hills."

Cheri knelt beside her and helped fold the fabric. "Not tonight," she said gently. "Tonight I just want quiet."

Patty studied her face, saw something she didn't recognize, and nodded. "All right. Quiet it is."

They finished their small chores, banked the fire, and went to their beds. The night outside was clear and cold; stars burned like watchful eyes above the roof.

Cheri dreamed again.

At first, only fire—white, radiant, alive. The temple walls shuddered under light that came from within. People ran, not from terror but awe.

A man stood in the center, arms outstretched, light pouring through cracks in his chest where a mark burned like flame. His face was sorrow and mercy at once.

Then ashes fell like snow, and a single heart-shaped ember pulsed in the ruin.

A voice spoke through the fire:
He will be called the Destroyer.
But he is the Heart of the Dawn.

Cheri woke with tears on her cheeks. Moonlight washed the blanket in silver. Patty snored softly, unaware that prophecy had just breathed beside her.

Cheri pressed a trembling hand over her heart. "Then I'll find him," she whispered. "And I'll remind him who he really is."

Outside, the wind rose, carrying the scent of northern pines. It slipped through the shutters and brushed her hair like a benediction.

When morning came, the bed across from Patty's was empty. The blanket was folded neatly. Cheri's pendant was gone from its hook by the window. Only the faint warmth of tea left cooling on the table remained—an apology in silence.

Patty stepped outside, early light pale over the fields. She looked toward the northern road, a ribbon of mist already swallowing its traveler.

"If you're wrong, Cheri," she whispered, "I'll forgive you. But if you're right…"
Her voice broke.
"…then I'll never forgive myself for not believing."

The wind caught her words and carried them north toward the rising sun.

Chapter Two — The Lesson of Suffering

"When discipline forgets compassion, it becomes cruelty wearing virtue's face."

The Road of Obedience

Dawn broke dull and gray over Stoneward Reach, as if even the sun hesitated to rise on a land so proud of its restraint. Frost rimed the courtyard stones; every sound seemed smaller for fear of echoing.

Joe paused on the dormitory steps, fingers brushing the scar beneath his collarbone—the raised mark that pulsed faintly with remembered light. All he had ever wanted was to be good—good enough for the Temple, good enough for the world, good enough for the light he barely understood.

They said it was a blessing, the Temple's mercy made

flesh.

They said mercy without control burned worlds.

He had believed them.

Most days.

He lowered his hand quickly, ashamed to seek comfort in something sacred. The small lantern at his belt—plain, practical—gave more warmth than the Temple's prayers ever did.

Leron waited near the gate, cloak drawn tight, breath fogging. His half-smile meant worry pretending not to be.

"You're late," he said.

"Barely. Kitchen boy cut his hand again—bread before doctrine."

Leron sighed. "You'll never learn detachment."

"He was bleeding," Joe said simply.

Leron studied him like a river that refused to freeze. "You can't ease every hurt."

"No," Joe answered. "But I can ease the ones I touch."

Something softened in Leron's eyes before duty shuttered it. "Come. Elder Maldrin wants us in Bracken Hollow. The well's rusted again."

At the name, Joe's stomach knotted. He pushed it down—obedience, humility, acceptance—the pillars of the Temple. Doubt was failure. Or so he'd been taught.

They started down the frost-dusted path. Birds watched from bare branches, still as carved icons. Only their boots spoke.

"Leron," Joe said quietly, "have you ever heard something that felt like a memory but wasn't?"

"Voices again?"

"Not voices. A thought—kindness, spoken aloud."

"That seal protects you," Leron warned. "If it weakens—"

"I know." Too quickly. Too hollow.

"We'll tell the elders when we return," Leron said, gentler. "They'll see to it."

Joe nodded though the thought chilled him—examination, judgment, reminders of what he was. "If it's weakening, I should want it fixed."

"You should," Leron echoed, and the echo sounded like fear.

The Boy and the Well

Bracken Hollow woke slowly, as if the village preferred dreams. Smoke curled from low chimneys; frost clung to thatch like spun glass. The air smelled of bread and pine pitch.

Joe breathed it in—earth, work, life unmeasured by bells. It felt cleaner than the Temple's marble.

"The well is ahead," Leron murmured.

A boy stumbled from a doorway, bucket too large for his hands. Water sloshed out, soaking his boots. Fear crossed his face—not of loss, but punishment.

Joe moved without thought. He steadied the boy's trembling hands. "Easy. Fetching for your family?"

The child nodded.

"What's your name?"

"Rian."

"Well, Rian, even warriors slip. Help me refill it?"

The boy blinked—astonished that spilled water met kindness, not rebuke—and nodded.

A door banged open. The father appeared, shoulders broad, eyes hollow.
"What's this? Coddling him?"

"It was an accident," Joe said calmly.

"Trying doesn't fill barrels," the man snapped. "Discipline does."

"Discipline teaches strength," Joe said, "but mercy teaches courage. We need both."

The man scoffed but turned away muttering.

Rian's small hand slipped into Joe's. Trust—simple and whole.

The scar beneath Joe's collarbone warmed, not with heat but recognition, like memory brushing truth.

A whisper, soft as breath over water: Gentleness is strength the world forgets.

The Water and the Watching

Joe froze. He didn't hear the words—he felt them, carved across his soul like sunlight through mist.

Leron noticed. "The seal?"

"I'm fine," Joe lied.

They reached the well. Villagers gathered in a cautious half-circle. A woman stepped forward clutching a jug. "Sir, they say the water's turning again."

Joe knelt. The bucket came up shimmering red with iron and neglect.

A watchman barked, "Put that down. Faith purifies; trials strengthen."

Joe straightened. "Children drink this. Faith shouldn't poison them."

"Pain chastens arrogance," the man retorted. "Nothing happens without holy purpose."

Joe's pulse quickened. He'd heard those words used to excuse too much.

"Suffering may teach," he said, "but kindness guides."

The crowd stirred—the sound of fear loosening its grip.

Leron stepped close. "We came to observe, not interfere."

"I know," Joe whispered. Yet his heart said otherwise.

The woman's hand brushed his sleeve—a plea, a blessing. He couldn't heal the water, not here, not yet—but he could give her dignity.

Hope flickered like a match cupped against wind.

The walk back began in silence. Frost cracked underfoot. A crow took wing—black against the pale sky.

Behind them, villagers moved a little lighter, as though someone had cracked a shutter to let dawn inside.

The Inn of Ash and Dawn

Joe tried not to look back. Hope made disobedience feel holy.
He was not allowed to think that.

Halfway up the rise he paused, looking down at the roofs and smoke and the small boy chasing frost. His heart tightened until it hurt.

The Temple taught that suffering purified.
All he saw were people trying to survive it.

Heat stirred low under his ribs—not rage, but fierce protectiveness. The scar throbbed once, bright, alive.

For one breath—one impossible, blasphemous breath—he did not fear it.
He wanted to defend, to heal, to burn away what hurt them.

Light flickered beneath his skin.

"Joe?" Leron's voice.

The fear returned like cold water. Joe clenched his fists, forcing the warmth down. The light faded.

"I'm fine," he managed.

Leron didn't believe him. "We'll tell the elders everything."

Joe nodded, dread hollowing his stomach. "Yes. Everything."

At the tree line, wind moved through branches though the air was still. A single silver strand of hair—Tess's—caught on bark and shimmered before drifting away.

He didn't see it.
But he paused anyway, unsure why his chest felt heavy and his eyes stung.

He exhaled, steadying himself. Duty first. Questions later.

He lifted his lantern—its fragile flame swaying like a mortal echo of something greater—and followed Leron back toward the Temple that would soon tremble under its own cruelty.

He didn't remember choosing to leave.
One moment he walked behind Leron; the next, the trees had closed around him, and the path bent toward the lowlands.

By dusk he reached the inn at the crossing—an old place with a sagging sign and the smell of woodsmoke and rain. The keeper, kind-eyed, handed him a key without questions.

Joe ate little; the bread turned to dust in his mouth. When he lay down, the straw mattress creaked beneath him, every sound reminding him how long it had been since silence wasn't an order but a gift.

Outside, the wind shifted, carrying the faint scent of iron—the memory of Bracken Hollow's well.

He sat up, pressing his hand to his chest. The scar was cool again, pretending it had never burned.

He remembered Rian's hand in his, the woman's tired eyes, the watchman's certainty.
He remembered mercy and how heavy it sounded when spoken aloud.

The Temple taught that mercy required control. Tonight, control felt like cowardice.

Joe exhaled, long and shaking. He wasn't sure if he prayed or confessed when he whispered, "If this is wrong, then let me be wrong in kindness."

The candle flickered. For a moment, the flame leaned toward him—like a friend trying to answer—but then it steadied.

He slept little. When dawn broke gray again, he rose, washed his face, and looked at the road stretching back toward Stoneward Reach.

He knew what waited: questions, judgment, Maldrin's pale eyes.
But he also knew he couldn't keep walking away from what he had seen.

He fastened the lantern to his belt. The glass caught the first pale light and reflected it back as something gentler.

"I'll face them," he murmured. "I won't let fear decide what mercy means."

Then he turned toward the road home—the one that would end in ruin before it led to grace.

Chapter Three — The Weight of Obedience

"When fear becomes law, even truth is treated as rebellion"

The Failing Seal

The reliquary beneath Stoneward Reach breathed like a held prayer.

Blue fire trembled in rune-cut braziers; the air smelled of iron and incense.

Maldrin stood in the center, hands on his staff. Its headpiece—an iron cage around a shard of crystal—should have shone like a captured sun.

Tonight it glimmered faintly, a candle where a star once burned.

He spoke the invocation.

"Covenant of control, seal of the faithful, receive."

Nothing.
Then a sluggish pulse—weak, late.

He inhaled sharply and tried again. Sparks leapt, then died. The chamber dimmed.

"The seal does not fade," he whispered, as if the air might agree. But the draw felt thin.
The boy.
Something in the boy had shifted.

For ten years the sigil had fed him steady warmth—wild mercy filtered through obedience. A perfect balance. Until now.

He turned to the obsidian mirror. His reflection looked thinner, more human than he liked.

"Mercy sickens when unbound," he said aloud. "If the seal weakens, the contagion spreads."

No answer came.

He straightened his robes, forced the tremor from his hands, and looked toward the spiral stair.
"He's slipping," he murmured. "And if he slips too far, the world forgets its order."

He quenched the braziers one by one. The crystal dimmed to ash.

"Find him," he said to the dark. "Bring him back. We'll remind mercy who holds its leash."

♥ ✳ ♥ ✳ ♥

Whispers in the Courtyard

At dawn, the gates of Stoneward Reach groaned open. Joe stepped through, frost clinging to his cloak.

The city beyond was as he remembered—clean, measured, silent. Even the bells rang without conviction, rituals echoing themselves.

Apprentices hurried across the square, scrolls tucked tight, eyes down. No one met his gaze. Not since the mark.

He crossed beneath the arch carved with the Covenant's creed:
Order Through Obedience. Peace Through Control.

He had read those words since boyhood. Today they felt heavier—like warning instead of welcome.

Inside, blue glass light made the marble shimmer like frozen water. At each doorway, voices hushed.

Leron waited near the refectory, shadows under his eyes. "They've been waiting for you."

"The Council?"

He nodded. "Maldrin returned early. Asked for you by name."

A shiver ran through Joe. "He knows about Bracken Hollow."

"They all know," Leron said softly. "Some call it mercy. Some call it disobedience. I told them you acted with compassion."

"That won't help," Joe murmured. "They don't value compassion."

Leron hesitated. "The High Prior's been restless. They say the reliquary flame dims."

Joe looked up sharply. "Dimmed?"

"He blames you."

Joe exhaled. "Then let him ask me himself."

They walked the long hall toward the Council Chamber. Murals of saints taming storms lined the walls—each a sermon in stone: power only holy when chained.

The Interrogation

Joe's footsteps echoed too loudly. His lantern swayed at his belt, casting brief warmth across the marble.

"Joe," Leron whispered at the doors, "choose your words carefully. They've already chosen theirs."

"I've no words left," Joe said. "Only truth."

The doors opened. Incense and judgment breathed out together.

Maldrin stood beneath the high window, light spilling over him like borrowed grace. The staff's crystal glowed weakly beneath his sleeve.

Joe bowed—respect for the office, not the man. "You sent for me, High Prior."

Maldrin's smile was patient, his tone almost kind. "Indeed, my son. I wish to understand."

"Understand what?"

"Where the power has gone."

Joe blinked. "Power?"

"The Covenant's light," Maldrin said, turning the staff so the faint glimmer winked like an eye. "It wanes. When the faithful weaken, the world weakens. Tell me, Joseph—what did you do in Bracken Hollow?"

"I listened."

Maldrin's smile didn't falter, but his eyes hardened. "To whom?"

"To suffering."

A murmur rippled through the elders.

Maldrin lifted a hand. Silence. "And what did suffering say?"

Joe met his gaze. "That holiness shouldn't depend on pain."

The chamber went still.

Maldrin felt the staff's hunger surge and fail. "You speak boldly, child."

"I speak plainly," Joe said. "If mercy needs permission, it isn't mercy."

The crystal flickered, a spark of gold leaping then dying. Maldrin felt the loss like pain.

"Plainly," he repeated, voice turning cold, "is how pride begins."

Joe felt pressure gather—the air tightening before judgment. The seal burned beneath his tunic, a heart remembering it was alive.

He straightened. "If mercy is pride, then I'll gladly be proud."

Gasps.

Leron stepped forward. "Joe—"

Too late.

Light coiled around the staff. The siphon reached for what it thought was its own.

Joe's scar flared, white light bursting through cloth. The crystal screamed like glass under strain.

Maldrin staggered. "No—"

The seal tore—not in blood or flame, but in sound: the world exhaling after ten years of held breath.

Joe arched as light poured from him, filling every corner of the hall. Elders fell, blinded. Leron covered his face, shouting his name.

Maldrin stumbled back. The siphon turned on its master—gold draining from the crystal into the air, seeking its true source. His robes caught light and burned in streaks.

He cried out once—not in pain, but disbelief—as the staff erupted. The blast hurled him backward through the stained-glass window.
Color shattered.
Light swallowed him whole.

When it faded, nothing remained—no shadow, no ash. Only the molten base of the staff cooling on the dais.

Silence followed—heavy, absolute.

Joe knelt amid ruin, breath ragged, the mark on his chest glowing faintly—no longer a geometric sigil but a raw flame-shaped wound beating with his pulse.

Leron crawled to him. "Joe… what have you done?"

Joe's voice came small, dazed. "Set them free."

He looked at his trembling hands, at the dust glittering in the sunlight. "All I wanted was mercy."

Outside, the forest wind carried the first cry of frightened bells.
And the Temple—once the heart of obedience—breathed its last.

When sound returned, it was dust settling. Columns lay cracked like ribs. The floor was veined with faintly glowing fissures.

Joe staggered upright. The air smelled of rain that hadn't fallen.

Bodies stirred—living ones. Apprentices, servants, elders. Unburned, untouched. Only the dais remained blackened.

Leron knelt beside the broken staff. "He's gone," he whispered. "All of it—gone."

Joe looked at the survivors. "No," he said softly. "Not all."

He stepped toward the doorway, bare feet streaking ash across the marble. The scar still glimmered through torn fabric—no longer geometry, only flame.

"Joe, wait," Leron called. "They'll call it heresy—"

"They already did." Joe's voice was calm. "And maybe they were right."

"Where will you go?"

He looked toward the horizon framed by shattered stone. "Where mercy isn't a crime."

He turned and walked into the dawn, each footstep echoing like a heartbeat against hollow walls.

Behind him, voices rose—broken, fearful.

"He did this," someone whispered. "The Devourer returned."

"Look at his mark—fire in the shape of a heart. The Destroyer walks again."

The word spread like smoke through the ruined halls. Destroyer.

It clung to the air even as Joe's figure faded down the road.

From the forest edge, Tess watched, hood drawn against the wind. Her knees trembled with the echo of power that wasn't hers.

Every soul still breathing in those ruins had been spared by Joe's light. She saw the pattern—the protective weave dissolving like wings into dust.

"He did it," she whispered. "He chose mercy."

A silver strand fell from her braid, glinting once before vanishing.

She pressed her palm against the bark of an old cedar. "Keep them safe," she murmured. The tree hummed in answer.

When she looked again, Joe was a silhouette against the morning fire, already small on the road.

"Run if you must," she said softly. "The dawn will find you again."

In the village below, bells tolled the ruin. Rumors took shape in mouths that had never seen the light itself.

The Devourer has risen.
The Temple burned by his hand.
The world trembles again.

Tess closed her eyes. "So it begins," she said. "They'll call him Destroyer until they learn the name he was born to bear."

The wind carried that name through the broken valley—
Heart of the Dawn.

Chapter Four — The River Between

"Two prayers spoken in different tongues can still seek
the same truth."

The House of Janis

Morning found Cheri weary from thinking too long about the miles ahead. The road from the village to Janis's homestead wound through wheatfields and stone; cart wheels hummed softly in the cold air.

By midday the clouds lowered, and woodsmoke rose ahead—Janis and Michael's cottage at the gate, hands raw from wind, pride thinner than warmth.

Inside, bread and woodsmoke greeted her. Michael stacked logs; Janis stirred herbs.

"Back so soon?" he teased.
"Maybe I was afraid to stop," she said.
Janis smiled. "Then rest first, think later."

They spoke of fences, frost, Patty's letters. But silence carried heavier questions. Cheri's eyes drifted to a small wooden box on the mantle.

Janis lifted the lid. "A traveler left this long ago. She said I'd know when to pass it on."

Inside lay a small half-circle of metal etched with faint runes that caught the light like ice over water.

"She said when it finds its match, the world will remember what it forgot."

Janis placed it in Cheri's hand. "I think it was waiting for you."

Warmth pulsed through the metal.

"Follow your heart," Janis whispered. "It hasn't lied yet."

Rain scented the wind as Michael packed bread and apples for her. Janis called, "Remember—don't lose yourself in the remembering."

Cheri nodded, the pendant warm against her skin, and turned toward the valley road.

The River of Guilt

Joe followed the river to a patch of blackened ground where reeds jutted like ribs. Guilt tightened his throat.

He knelt, opening his palm over the ash. "If mercy still lives in me, prove it."

Light gathered—then burst. When it cleared, the soil had fused to glass. Steam curled from his hands.

"This is what they meant," he whispered. "Untamed mercy devours."

The mark on his chest flared red-gold. He tore his cloak across it, trembling. "I am the Devourer."

The pendant at his wrist throbbed once in answer. He shoved it into his pack. "No more prayers."

He stripped away his robes, wrapped himself in a traveler's cloak, and walked north beside the river, a single dim lantern at his belt.

Behind him, the scorched ground flickered once—light trying to breathe through glass—but he never looked back.

♥ ✳ ♥ ✳ ♥

The Call Across Water

Night came quiet.
Far apart yet bound by the same current, two souls
paused beside the river.

Cheri

She knelt at the bank, the half-sigil glowing
faintly. Cold water kissed her fingers like an old
memory aching to return to touch. "If he's lost," she
whispered, "let mercy find him first."

Light bloomed—a face forming in the ripples,
eyes bright with grief and fire and something she knew
at once: a light that refused to die.

Her breath caught. "Heart of the Dawn…
you're real."

The voice that reached her was more feeling
than sound:
You should run. I will ruin you.

She shook her head. "No. I'll remind you who
you are."

The water stilled, leaving only her reflection—
faith fierce enough to challenge fate itself.

Joe

Upstream, sleepless, he dipped his hand into the same current. Water glowed; a woman's face formed in the water, her lips shaping his name.

He jerked back. "No—stay away."

Her thought brushed his mind:
You are not the destroyer.

Pain seared through the scar; light shattered across the river. "Don't come near me," he gasped. "If you do, I'll burn you too."

He clutched the hidden pendant. "Let the curse end with me."
The glow faded.

The River

Miles apart, they sat under one moon.
For a heartbeat the river between them glowed gold, then quieted—like a promise keeping its breath.

On a high ridge, Tess watched, silver hair catching moonlight. The prayer left her trembling but smiling.

"They've seen each other," she whispered. "The song begins."

Below, the river carried their light into the dark, the first verse of something that would not end.

Chapter Five — Faith In Motion

"Faith walks where fear has already built a road."

Ashvale Arrival

The sun crept low and wide across the hills when Joe first saw the village — a ring of cottages wrapped around a crooked square, smoke rising from uneven chimneys. He'd hoped for quiet, for bread, for something to make him feel like a man again instead of a ruin.

The name carved on the well post read Ashvale. He almost laughed at the irony.

He'd traded his temple robes for a plain traveler's cloak, though the cut of his stride still marked him as someone used to order. The satchel at his hip hid the pendant. The mark beneath his shirt — the still-tender flame scar — throbbed faintly, but he kept his hand away from it. People could smell fear, and he reeked of it.

At the baker's stall, he offered a few coins for bread. The woman's eyes flicked to the faint reddish glow under his collar, just visible where his tunic had torn. She froze.

"You—" she whispered. "Your chest—"

Joe glanced down, too late. The scar had flared in the heat. A pulse of gold light flickered through the cloth.

A man nearby dropped his pail. "It's him," he hissed. "The one from Stoneward Reach. The Devourer."

Voices rose like startled birds.
Someone spat. A child began to cry.

"I'm not—" Joe started, but his throat closed around the lie. Not what? Not cursed? Not guilty?

A young priest pushed through the gathering crowd — all white linen and trembling authority. "Show us your mark," he demanded. "If it is sanctified, we'll see the sign."

Joe took a step back. "Please. I only want to pass through."

"Remove your cloak," the priest said, hand tightening on a small iron talisman.

Joe hesitated — and that was all it took. The baker screamed. The crowd surged. Fear needed no proof; it needed only a spark.

He turned to run, but the priest lunged forward and grabbed his arm. Pain seared through Joe's chest. The mark answered with light — a reflex, not an act. Fire licked the air between them, brief and bright as a heartbeat. The priest stumbled back, clutching his burned hand.

The crowd roared.
"Destroyer!" someone shouted. "He'll burn us all!"

Joe fled. Stones struck his back, boots pounding dirt, shouts chasing him out beyond the last row of cottages. He didn't stop until he reached the far field where the first frost was settling, breath tearing in his lungs.

He fell to his knees beside a half-frozen ditch, retching on air. "You see?" he rasped to the night. "You see what I am?"

The scar glowed once more, faintly softer this time, as if trying to answer.
He covered it with both hands. "Don't," he whispered. "Don't pity me."

He found an abandoned barn and collapsed inside, too tired to think, too ashamed to pray.
When he finally slept, the wind outside sounded like the low hum of the temple bell — but no one was calling him home.

By the next afternoon, Ashvale had gone gray under drizzle. Cheri's cloak was soaked by the time she reached the village edge. She had followed the river road since dawn, guided by the warmth of the pendant against her chest and the strange certainty that she was walking the right way.

The first thing she noticed was the silence.
Windows shuttered. Doors half-closed. Fear hung heavier than the rain.

At the well, two women whispered as she approached. She caught only fragments — "fire," "burned mark," "the Destroyer."

Cheri set her pack down gently. "What happened here?"

The older woman eyed her warily. "A man came through yesterday. Sayimg he was hungry. We saw the flame under his shirt. He burned the priest's hand for trying to help him."

The Confrontation

Cheri frowned. "Did he threaten you?"

"No," the younger one admitted, "but he carried a curse. You could feel it."

Cheri let the silence breathe for a long moment. "Fire isn't always a curse," she said softly. "It's how the dawn begins."

The older woman scowled. "That's dangerous talk."

"Maybe." Cheri smiled faintly. "But maybe dangerous faith is still faith."

She left them whispering and walked through the square. Near the well she found a patch of scorched ground

— small, circular, as if lightning had kissed it. She knelt beside it and touched the edge.

Warm.
Not burning. Just alive.

Grass pushed through the cracks — thin green blades curling from what should have been dead earth. She closed her eyes. The image of the frightened man from her river vision filled her mind. He hadn't looked wicked; he'd looked wounded.

She whispered to the ground, "You're not the Destroyer. You're the one who forgot his own mercy."

When she stood again, the rain had eased. A child watched her from a doorway — the same boy who had cried when Joe fled. She smiled and handed him a piece of dried fruit from her satchel. He hesitated, then took it. His mother pulled him close but said nothing.

Cheri walked on. Behind her, the child turned back to look — and the burned patch at the well glowed faintly, as if remembering light.

Chapter Six — The Rust and the Ravens

"Rumor feeds on silence more than on truth."

♥ ✳ ♥ ✳ ♥

The Ruins and the Ravens

The air above the ruins still shimmered faintly, as though the fire refused to surrender its memory. Leron stood at the crest of the hill where the temple bell had fallen and split, its bronze mouth cracked like an unanswered prayer. Ash drifted with every gust—white, gray, and faintly gold where molten glass had cooled in the dust. Even the ground seemed uncertain whether to mourn or rest.

The ravens had come first. Dozens of them— black-eyed, cold-minded birds that witnessed the end of men without offering grief. They strutted across shattered stone, plucking at scraps of cloth and fragments of parchment that the wind refused to bury.

One perched atop the broken cistern and cried out, its hoarse call echoing down the valley like a verdict.

Leron drew his cloak tighter. The ground still radiated a dull warmth, the kind that felt more like memory than flame. He passed the line where apprentices once stood each dawn—stone worn smooth by hundreds of bare heels learning reverence long before they ever learned rebellion. In the smoke's shifting hush, he could almost hear their laughter again—faint, impossible, gone.

He had buried too many of them already. The rest—he wasn't sure. Some had fled before the light fell. Others had vanished inside the white blaze Joe had unleashed. None had returned.

He wanted to be angry with Joe. It would be easier to call him what the elders now called him—Destroyer—and leave it at that. Easier than believing mercy could end in ruin.

A glint near the fallen dormitory caught his eye. Kneeling, he brushed aside ash and uncovered a half-burned book bound in temple cloth. The sigil had blistered away, but the spine held.

Inside, the first pages crumbled. The next had survived.

The handwriting—hurried, uneven, painfully human—was Joe's. Leron had corrected those letters enough times to recognize every stubborn stroke.

He read:

Mercy is not weakness. If the Light is love, why do we chain it? They teach that discipline is holiness, yet I have seen another truth in dream. A woman of light said power that heals cannot be corrupted. Perhaps it was only my mind. But the dream felt truer than their sermons.

A drop—tear or water—had bled the ink at the edge.

The wind turned a page.

Maybe the world does not need more chains. Maybe it needs remembering.

Leron shut the book. Ash streaked his hands, dark as guilt.

The smashed statue of the Covenant lay nearby, marble feet scattered like broken commandments.

"I taught him obedience," he whispered. "But he learned mercy instead."

A raven hopped closer, head tilted as if waiting for confession.

"Maybe mercy remembers even when faith forgets," he murmured.

He tucked the journal into his cloak and rose. Somewhere in the distance, a hammer struck wood— the rhythm of rebuilding, or burial. The world was already moving on.

Ravens spiraled upward, turning the weak morning light silver for a heartbeat.

Leron bowed his head. "If you live, boy… don't let them teach you to hate what made you kind."

He walked away, leaving footprints in the ash for the wind to claim.

The Ash-Stained Road

The road bent through fields that no longer remembered color. Frost and char shared the soil. Last season's dead wheat rattled like bones in the wind.

Cheri drew her cloak close and whispered her morning prayer—habit, hope, or both: Guide the heart that seeks, even when it fears what it will find.

Far ahead, heat haze wavered above a cold horizon. At a crossroads, a lone traveler approached with the gait of someone unsure whether he was leaving something behind or running from it.

Leron's staff struck the stones in a slow, tired rhythm.

As they neared one another, he raised a hand in greeting. "Not many travel north this time of year," he said, voice worn thin.

"Faith doesn't ask the season," Cheri replied—sharper than intended. She softened. "I heard the roads near Stoneward are closed. Is it true?"

He hesitated. The answer carried weight beyond the words. "Closed," he said. "Or cursed, if you listen to rumor. The temple… fell."

"I've heard." She paused. "Some say a Devourer did it."

Grief flickered behind his disciplined expression. "A word for things we don't understand."

He looked at her fully, measuring her sincerity. "I was there when it burned."

Cheri's heart stilled—not in fear, but recognition. "What happened?"

"Light," he said. "Too much of it. The priests called it judgment. I think…" His voice faltered. "I think it was mercy no one knew how to receive."

Ash lifted from his cloak, swirling around them like dull snow.

"You speak as if you knew the one they blame," she said gently.

"I knew a boy." His gaze drifted north. "Kind. Too kind for the shape they tried to press him into." He scraped a small circle in the dust with his staff. "Sometimes kindness sets fires rules can't contain."

Cheri swallowed. Her dreams returned—light in ruins, a voice crying through flame: He isn't the Destroyer. He's the Heart of the Dawn. Her fingers trembled around her satchel.

"Maybe the world fears mercy because it can't command it," she said.

Surprise cracked the man's grim composure. For a moment, they simply stood in the crossroads wind—guilt facing faith.

"You speak like someone I once failed to listen to," he said.

"And you," she answered, "like someone still trying to make amends."

A faint smile touched his lips—worn, wanting, sincere. "Perhaps we walk the same road."

"Only one of us knows where it ends," she replied.

"Do you?"

"I'll know when I find the one I'm meant to."

They walked together until the road narrowed between blackened poplars. Neither spoke—the silence felt like a pause between questions no one yet knew how to ask.

At last he stopped by a collapsed milestone. Gently, he set down his pack.

"There's something I was meant to carry," he said. "Perhaps it was never meant for me."

He withdrew a warped, soot-stained book. Gold ink glimmered faintly under the burn marks.

Cheri's breath caught. "You saved it?"

"It saved me," he murmured. "When the temple fell, I thought I was finished with faith. But these pages…" His fingers brushed the cover. "They didn't preach. They wrestled. They hoped."

He held the journal out. "You sound like him."

Cheri hesitated, then accepted it reverently. The cover was warm—almost breathing. When she opened to the first surviving page, the ink shimmered softly:

Mercy is not weakness. If the Light is love, why do we chain it?

Her heart tightened. "He writes like someone pleading and fighting with fate at the same time."

"Then you understand him better than most," the man said. "If you find him… tell him I was wrong."

Before she could reply, he shouldered his pack, turned south, and vanished into the drifting ash.

Cheri clutched the journal to her chest. "I will find him," she whispered. "Not to condemn him… but to remind him."

Far on the horizon, something pulsed faintly—too brief for anyone without faith to notice.

♥ ✳ ♥ ✳ ♥

The Night of the Journal

Cheri found shelter where the scorched fields gave way to pale birch trees. She built a small fire and set the journal across her knees.

The pages breathed with life—ink uneven, smoke-warped edges curling like autumn leaves. She brushed soot from the margin and read:

I fear what I carry, yet it sings when I'm kind.

She touched the line with trembling fingers.

They say compassion softens. But it is the only thing that doesn't break me.

She closed the book, holding it against her heart as if it might spill if left open too long.

A spark snapped in the fire. For a heartbeat she thought she saw a figure of pale hair watching from the trees. When she blinked, only ash drifted.

"Who are you?" she whispered.

The birches whispered back—a breath, not a wind.

The journal slid open in her lap as if guided by memory rather than physics. A new page rested flat.

There is a girl I dream of. I never see her face, only her voice. She says my name as if she's finding it.

Cheri's breath caught. "I am looking for you, too," she whispered.

She banked the fire and curled beneath her cloak. In sleep she dreamed of a man kneeling beside a ruined well, mercy bleeding through his hands like light.

At dawn she woke with one vow on her lips: "I will find him."

Miles north, as Joe stirred awake in a roadside inn, the scar beneath his collarbone pulsed once—soft, steady, like a heart remembering it had never stopped.

Chapter Seven — Dreams of Ash and Light

"Two souls can mistake prophecy for memory."

Moonlit Water and Memory

The inn had no name, only a hanging board that creaked in the wind where paint used to be. Beyond it, a stream threaded through frost-bitten reeds, silver where the moon touched it and black where it slipped under alder roots. Joe came down the slope long after the laughter in the common room had gone quiet and the last candle had guttered out with a soft hiss. His boots sank a little in the soft bank. The smell of wet earth and old smoke clung to everything.

He knelt and let the night press close, as if it might squeeze the ache out of him. The mark beneath his collarbone pulsed—duller now than in the first hours after the temple fell, but relentless, like a memory that refuses to be rewritten. It wasn't geometry anymore. The crisp lines of the sigil had melted into a flame-shaped wound whose edges curled as though the skin remembered heat. He'd wrapped it in linen and then torn the linen away because he couldn't stand the bind—then wrapped it again, ashamed of the tremor in his hands.

"Order. Purity. Silence," he murmured, the old prayer tasting like dust.

The river did not care for silence. It spoke in small, tireless sentences—against stones, around roots, across the ankles of the grass where winter had not finished its argument. Joe dipped his fingers. Cold bit, then bloomed. Ripples went outward in neat rings and, strangely, came back—gathering toward his hand as if the water had changed its mind about which direction belonged to it.

He stared down. The moon fractured in the shallows, broke into pieces and mended itself again. For a second the face in the water wasn't quite his. The

mouth looked the same but the eyes held a steadiness
he had not felt in days. He blinked and it was gone. He
breathed and it returned—the same and not the
same—like a story told twice by someone who loved it
too much to keep the details still.

"Whatever I touch," he whispered to no one,
"learns to burn."

The Pool of Quiet Fire

South of that nameless inn, far from Janis's
orchard and the cottage she'd left behind, the river ran
thinner and faster. Cheri followed it by moonlight until
the rush softened into a pool edged with white-barked
birches. The ground there wore frost like lace. She laid
a small circle of stones, coaxed fire from a stubborn
nest of shavings, and held her hands out to the modest
flame as if it were a guest she meant to keep.

The journal rested on her knees, its spine warm
where her palms had remembered it all afternoon. The

edges were singed and the cover warped, but the ink inside lived—dark strokes and hurried letters that chose mercy over elegance and truth over neatness. She read the same line until the sounds went soft and the meaning went bright: Mercy runs toward fire, not away.

She closed the book and breathed so the words could settle where breath makes room for faith. Then she slid forward, palms on cold stone, and touched the pool.

At first, only cold—teeth of it, then the duller ache. Then the sensation softened into something like a held note. Ripples ran out in tidy rings and returned just as tidy, as if the night were practicing patience with her. Her reflection trembled and kept its shape. The trees leaned in, or seemed to. The fire made no sound. The world waited as if the next word belonged to her.

"I'm looking for someone," she told the water. "I think he's looking for me."

The pool did not answer except by stilling more deeply. She felt her own heartbeat in her fingers as a faint thrum. When she lifted her hand, the surface held the shape of it a moment longer than water usually allows.

Something in her rose like light through shutter cracks.

Reflections That Touch Light

The bank swallowed his words. The stream swallowed the bank. Somewhere a night bird called— three notes, patient as a teacher who believes in the slow work of listening.

He took his hand from the water and the cold left an ache that wasn't punishment so much as proof. He pressed his palm against the scar. Heat swelled. It hurt the way a confession hurts—cleanly.

He waited for the pain to decide what to become.

Joe cupped water and let it run off his knuckles, slower than it should. He noticed his breath—the way it refused to arrange itself into prayer—and, because he had learned to notice, he let the refusal be honest. The mark warmed under the linen. The warmth spread down his ribs and along the lines of old scars he rarely remembered earning.

He leaned. The stream leaned back. The reflection steadied. And then—

Not his face.

A woman, not beside him but somehow within the same pane of water, as if the river were a shared window. Her hair carried a sheen like the first breath of morning on frost; not gold, not silver—both and neither. Her gaze did not startle or accuse. It recognized. That recognition struck him lower than the mark.

He did not speak. He didn't know what name would answer him.

Her lips moved. Sound did not cross the water the way ordinary sound does. The meaning found him anyway, as if carried on something small and tireless that lives under meaning.

Who are you?

He meant not to answer. He meant to be wise in the way fear calls wisdom. But truth outran intent.

"I don't know anymore," he said, and the river took the shape of the words, smoothed them, sent them on.

Cheri flinched—not from fright, but from the tenderness of being believed by the world. The pool brightened along its center seam, as if something below it had smiled. The man in the water lifted his head as if it had suddenly grown lighter.

She saw the tiredness at the corners of his mouth and the unpracticed hope near his eyes. She saw the way his shoulders held their sorrow privately, the way gentle people often learn to carry their pain without making a spectacle of it.

"You're not what they call you," she said softly. The sentence trembled from certainty to mercy and landed as both.

His hand moved, then stilled. She saw the shadow of linen under his shirt and the way it rose and fell faster than resting breath.

"Then what am I?"

"The Heart of the Dawn."

When she said it, she did not mean time of day. She meant source. She meant first light that enters a room nobody remembered had windows. She meant warmth that chooses to belong to the cold it touches.

The pool brightened—as if agreeing. Her own reflection faded until only his remained, steadier now. She reached, and the water did not disagree with the idea of touch. The cold tug kissed her skin.

The scar flared like a struck match, then like the flame you cup so the wind will not humiliate it. Heat rolled outward, then returned, as if the body had become a bellows. He wanted the hand in the water. He wanted to hold it the way you hold a truth you have not earned but are nonetheless required to carry. He wanted—and the wanting terrified him because every lesson of the temple had taught him that desire is the door arrogance uses to enter.

"Stop," he said, the plea hurting his throat. "You'll burn."

She did not pull back. Her expression altered the smallest degree—more sorrow than pity, more courage than challenge. The water thickened between them, light pooling where their not-quite-touch found each other.

"You won't," she whispered. "You're light, not fire."

Light, not fire. He tried to believe. The mark heard the words and for an instant answered them—

heat shifting to warmth, sting to ache. And because he had never learned to receive mercy without arguing, he pulled away.

The vision shattered. Water leapt where his knee broke the reflection. Moon and bank and alder stripped the river back to what ordinary eyes call real.

He stumbled into the weeds and braced himself on roots that had done nothing to deserve a man's panic. He pressed a hand to the wound until his palm went damp and the bright edge of pain dulled into the familiar weight of it. He swallowed air until it remembered how to be useful.

"Whoever you are," he said to the indifferent dark, "don't find me."

Steps Toward Each Other

The river, professional and undeterred, continued being a river.

The pool held stillness longer than water should. When it loosed it at last, the surface unstitched the bright seam with care, as if returning a borrowed garment without creasing it. Cheri let her hand go slack. Cold dripped from her wrist into the moss. The birch trees along the bank made their pale little music, and the fire she'd built settled its small shoulders as if relieved to have performed beyond its size.

She looked down at the journal and found it open where she had not left it. A new line had appeared—ink dark and tender, edges still glistening as if written by breath rather than hand:
Mercy remembers.

She touched the words and felt—what? Not heat, not the prick of magic, nothing easy to name. Only the rightness she associated with prayer that does not ask for outcomes, only alignment.

"Then so will I," she said, and the sentence chose her mouth as its home for a while.

She banked the fire, gathered her pack, and stood. The night had softened at the horizon—no color yet, only the sense that color was about to exist. She faced north because north was what the dream had made hers.

He climbed the inn yard as the first tired rooster announced its sense of duty. Inside, straw tick and blanket waited, but he did not. He took the narrow stair two at a time, lifted the latch, entered the small room that smelled of soap and woodsmoke, and began to fold his life back into travel.

Bread, wrapped. Water, corked. Lantern, checked and hung where the chain knew the shape of his hip.

He chose a coarse shirt and pulled it over the linen bandages until the burn hid like a decision not yet admitted.

He looked at the bed and almost lay down. He looked at the door and chose the door. One of the inn's cats watched him from the far end of the hall with the unblinking charity of creatures who never confuse silence with judgment.

On the yard's edge he paused, not to reconsider but to tell himself, for later, why he was choosing to run: because he loved the world enough to get away from it while he was dangerous. Because he had learned that kindness sometimes means absence. Because a woman whose voice felt like dawn had reached for him, and if he let her finish the gesture, he would belong to something larger than his fear, and he was not sure who he was without the fear to define him.

He set his feet to the road and let the cold talk his knees into moving.

Cheri walked until the frost found her boot seams and pointed out their failures. She walked until the birch trees gave way to rocks that remembered glaciers and beyond them to pasture rough as a poor man's beard. She did not hurry. Faith rarely does.

When she grew tired enough to mistake stubbornness for virtue, she stopped and said the name she did not know in the way you are certain the world will remember on your behalf.

"Guide me," she said, which was both a request and a promise to listen.

The journal in her pack shifted, not enough to be miracle—enough to be company. She imagined, not unreasonably, that the man who wrote it had once said a prayer much like this and had meant it with a softness that frightened people who confused tenderness with weakness.

She smiled into a wind that did not earn the courtesy and kept going.

By mid-morning the road north from the nameless inn crossed a ridge where hawthorns held red berries like stubborn hope. Joe climbed until his breath dragged, then turned and looked back. The valley wore its smoke as lightly as it could. A heron took itself from one patch of water to another, legs unfolding like the careful greeting of an old friend. He closed his eyes, not to shut the world out, but to carry it with him better.

Far behind and southward, Cheri crested a low hill where the river made a slow-minded loop and let the sun have it. She shaded her gaze and squinted as if distance might answer to effort. Her chest tightened in the particular way that meant her heart had decided to be wise before the mind did.

Two breaths, separated by miles, found the same rhythm. Neither knew it, and both felt less alone.

That night, as the moon apprenticed itself to fullness again, the two rivers held the memory of being doors. They did not hurry to forget. Water has a way of filing things under eventually, which is not the same as never. Fish moved where light had once divided the surface; a fox drank right where warmth had once threaded two lives. Alder, birch, reed—they remembered in their particular fashions and told no one.

In sleep, Joe dreamed—not of fire, though the scar pulsed, but of a hand that had touched water and did not flinch when the cold spoke plainly. In waking, he would call it nonsense and feel steadier for the lie. In sleeping, he turned toward the dream like a man consenting to be warmed.

In sleep, Cheri dreamed—not of prophecy with trumpets, but of a room that had once believed itself windowless and now possessed a seam of light. She woke before dawn and did not wait for worry to speak first. She whispered a vow, because vows like to be spoken while the world is still quiet enough to hold them without dropping them.

"I will find you," she said. "Not to save you from yourself, but to remind you of yourself."

The morning took the sentence and set it beside a man's footsteps on a road that tried, as roads do, to be helpful without making promises it could not keep.

Chapter Eight — The Innocent and the Heretic

"Fear is faith that has forgotten its name."

Mercy in the Market

Brinvale clung to its hillside like a cat on a wet fence. Mist hugged the river bottom; smoke stitched crooked lines into a sky the color of bleached wool. By the time Cheri reached the stone bridge, the road had turned to a ribbon of mud polished by cart wheels and hurried shoes. She stopped long enough to shake thawing frost from her cloak and to listen. Markets announce themselves before you see them—tin clatter, a vendor's laugh turned bargaining, the soft drum of feet—and beneath it all the low, shared murmur of people deciding what they believe today.

She crossed into the square and let the crowd carry her a few steps. Stalls leaned together under sagging awnings: apples stacked like small suns, onions braided into pale ropes, a spice seller flicking red dust from a wooden scoop. Sawdust haloed the butcher's boots. Somewhere bread cracked in an oven and the smell made her knees go conversational. She smiled in spite of the chill, in spite of the ache that had taken up residence beneath her ribs since the river-vision. Joy didn't cancel longing; it companioned it.

"From the south?" asked a woman arranging jars of pickled carrots into a regiment of orange spears. Her accent stacked syllables like stones.

"Farther," Cheri said. "And farther yet to go."

The woman's eyes found the silver thread along the hem of Cheri's cloak and then darted away, as if respect were safer from the side. "Mind your tongue, then. There's been talk."

"There's always talk," Cheri said lightly, but she let the words pull more attention from the air than her tone did.

The woman leaned in until vinegar stung Cheri's eyes. "They say a man burned a temple to the ground with a thought, and some swear he drinks light out of wells. They call him Destroyer."

Cheri kept her face still. Devourer first, she corrected silently. Destroyer only after men chose fear over truth. Aloud she said, "Names are easy. Truth takes work."

"Work's in short supply," the woman sniffed, but she smiled; it softened her warning into care. "Buy onions. You can trust an onion."

Cheri laughed, bought two, and moved on, listening the way Janis had taught her: not only for words but for what bends them. Snatches reached her as she passed—a hawker swearing by his mother's teeth that the salt was from the true sea, not the marsh; boys trading rumors like marbles; a priest with a travel-stained stole collecting offerings for a chapel roof that wouldn't stay mended. The Destroyer lived in everyone's mouth but no two mouths held him the same shape.

"…spite, I tell you. He hated the Covenant and meant to shame it—"

"—mercy! My cousin says his boy breathed sweet after the light, not rust like before—"

"—witchcraft from the east. They have women there who sing storms—"

"—the High Prior's gone. Vanished. That's what power does when justice comes for it—"

Cheri let the threads tug at her and did not let them tie her. Her hand brushed her satchel—feeling for the weight of the journal the way a traveler checks for bread without meaning to. She had not read since last night, but knowing the words were near steadied her like a hand between her shoulders.

A shout cracked the square's hum.

She turned. Near the public fountain, where a cracked stone beast spat a thin runnel of water into a basin rimmed with old limescale, a small boy crouched beside a dog. The animal's paw bled bright onto the cobbles; the boy's scarf hung in a clumsy knot, nose running unchecked in the cold. He reached for the dog and the dog flinched, teeth showing and then ashamed of the showing.

"Leave it," someone called. "Filth carries curses." Another: "It's a sign. Bad luck since the burning—don't touch it." A third voice, lower and crueler: "Kick it off the stones and be done."

Cheri's feet moved before her thoughts caught up. She crouched, boots splashing in the shallow film around the basin, and pitched her voice the way you do when fear already has too much to listen to. "Easy. Both of you."

The boy looked up, eyes wider than a reasonable grief requires, and then looked down again, not at the dog but at the adult voices like they were hands coming from every direction. "He's mine," he said in the small voice of a person who is used to being contradicted. "Or if he isn't, he wants to be."

"Then he is," Cheri said, as if the sentence were obvious and older than law. "Hold him there." She tore a strip from the inside lining of her cloak—Michael's careful stitchwork twinged in her conscience and then yielded to the necessity—and pressed it against the paw. The dog whined and then, when she met his gaze and held it, stilled. She cleaned the wound with water cupped from the fountain and bound it firm. "You're brave," she told the boy, and meant both of them.

"You shouldn't do that." The priest with the travel-stained stole had stepped nearer. His insignia had once been gold, now a tired brass; the thread that held his stole to his collar had given up and was only pretending loyalty. He did not speak loudly, but the square learned to hear him. "Suffering sharpens faith. If the creature is marked, there's a lesson."

"What lesson?" Cheri asked without looking up. She didn't soften the question. Mercy doesn't always come in soft voices.

"That what is broken must await its appointed time," he returned, and liked the sound of his own answer enough to keep going. "We are a people of order, not of—of meddling. Pain chastens arrogance. We do not play at power with blood and bandage."

She tied the knot neatly, checked the dog's eyes again, then rose. The boy's hand found the dog's ear and stayed there as if permission had been granted for both. Cheri faced the priest. "Kindness is not pretending we hold all power. It's remembering we don't."

Murmurs swelled. Words like east and witch and meddler slithered into the warmer fabric of the crowd. A stone clinked against the basin's rim, more accident than threat—until it wasn't. The priest lifted his chin, drawing the square to a point. "Where did you learn to lay hands on curses?"

"In kitchens," she said. "In fields. At bedsides when the fever broke at last. From women who make stew and men who bury their pride. From a friend who said the right measure of mercy is whatever a human breath can carry."

"That is not doctrine," he said, scandal and triumph braided in his tone.

"It is practice," she answered.

A laugh, sharp and ugly, from the back. "Hear that? She talks like the forest witch. Like Tess."

The name moved through the air with the guilty magnetism of a sin people enjoy too much to repent.

Faces sharpened toward her. Tess meant east; east meant heresy; heresy meant the crowd could call cruelty courage and admire itself for it. Cheri felt heat at her cheeks and let it stand—shame is useless here; anger can serve if it remembers it's a tool and not a home.

She lifted her hands so everyone could see they were empty. "I don't ask you to believe me," she said. "Just—look." She tipped her head toward the boy. He had tucked his leaking nose into his sleeve and was failing to be brave in the way children fail when they have not had practice at anything else. The dog leaned against him the measured distance that says we can share weight if you'd like. "He is less afraid now than he was a minute ago. The dog is, too. If either of those strike you as a problem, then the problem isn't me."

A woman near the fruit stall made a sound that wasn't quite agreement and wasn't quite nerves. "She bound it like my mother did," she said to no one, to everyone. "Same knot."

"Same knot," someone echoed, and then the spell of the priest's certainty loosened a finger.

The priest recovered, as men schooled in rightness do. "Compassion is not a license. We have forms." He held up a palm as if to bless or to fend—sometimes the same gesture does both. "There are trials that purify a town. We do not steal them away."

"Ah," Cheri said, and let her voice be soft now because a soft voice can be the sharpest tool when it is the last thing anyone expects. "So you would rather a child learn to swallow his cry than a village learn to share it."

He reddened. "You will not preach here."

"I won't," she said, and meant it. "But I will stay."

A stone rolled under her boot—the same one, or a new one testing its courage. She saw the thrower now: a man with a face like winter—nothing personal in it, only season. His hand trembled less from malice than from the wish to belong to whichever group wins. It is a wish that has cost more goodness than any doctrine. He crouched to pick it up again and stood, weight settling with decision.

Cheri's mouth went dry. She did not move. Fear has a way of splashing everywhere when you jostle it.

Better to stand still and let it run off your boots. She thought of Patty's hands around a mug, knuckles whitening when the argument about faith and sense had come to the familiar bend. She thought of Janis's smile, that slow, stern tenderness that says I will not untie you from your heart even if it would be easier for both of us. She thought of a river that had once chosen to be a door.

The man drew his arm back.

"Don't," Cheri said—not loud, just true.

Something in the square paused. It could have gone either way. People love to be caught by a new wind. People love to prove they cannot be moved. She did not know which love would win.

Then the boy—blessed and small with unscheduled courage—stood up. "She helped him," he said. He did not shout. He did not plead. "She helped him."

The dog chose its unsteady feet and, with the stubborn dignity dogs reserve for children, put its bandaged paw down and did not yelp. It leaned against the boy's shin like a vote.

"Same knot," the fruit-seller repeated, louder now, making it an offering. "My mother's knot."

"Same," echoed someone else, and the word took on the weight of a chorus line.

The stone-thrower's arm lowered. He looked embarrassed by his own theater and then resentful at the embarrassment. The priest's mouth opened to rally and found no place to land.

Cheri let out a breath she hadn't invited into her chest in the first place. She crouched again to meet the boy's eyes. "You did well," she said. "Keep him warm today. Tomorrow, if the paw smells sour or he keeps it off the ground, you'll need vinegar and boiled cloth. Ask the carrot-seller." She smiled toward the woman, who drew herself up into a posture she'd always secretly wanted to practice—public competency. "She knows knots."

The woman sniffed, but her hands had already begun to tidy jars that did not need tidying in the way people tidy when their heart is busy accepting a job.

A bell began to toll from the chapel tower on the hill—the hour, or the habit of the hour. It sounded slightly off, as if it had been forged to another town's idea of time and never forgiven it. The square started to breathe again. Prices reasserted themselves. Someone remembered a song. The priest, seeing the moment gone to earth, gathered his stole around his throat and retreated toward safer devotions.

Cheri rose, legs shaking now that no one required their steadiness. She stroked the dog once along the skull; it licked the bandage because gratitude is clumsy in every species. The boy smiled, which hurt the morning in a good way.

As she turned away, a voice behind her—low, travel-worn—said, "You shouldn't linger when fear is bored. It finds work."

She looked back only far enough to register a figure at the edge of the square, staff in hand, dust on his hem, eyes that knew too much about gentleness. He did not step closer. He did not name himself.

"I have work of my own," Cheri said.

"North, then," the figure answered, and the word held both warning and blessing. "But not alone."

She blinked and a cart rolled between them, a slap of reins and the ache of a mule accepting a poor argument. When the way cleared, the man was gone— as if he had not been there, or as if the square had decided to keep him for later.

Cheri stood very still until stillness felt like a decision rather than a default. She bought bread she did not want because part of courage is feeding it. She tied the onions to her pack with a length of twine the pickle-seller pressed into her palm as if the gesture could erase vinegar between them. She checked the journal with a hand that wanted to be seen doing it and then didn't pull it out, because not everything needs a witness to be true.

Only when she reached the far side of the square did she allow herself to look back. The boy sat with his dog beside the fountain. The bandage held. The priest had found a widow to bless. The fruit-seller stood a little taller. The bell tolled again, and this time, she thought, it sounded closer to in tune.

Cheri turned her face toward the north road. The rumors would run ahead of her the way rumors do, inventing new names for the same old fear—forest-witch, heretic, destroyer's bride. Let them run. Faith walks. It arrives.

She stepped off the square and into the thin street where laundry lines dared the wind to argue. Behind her, someone said softly, not to her, not for her, but because some sentences require speaking to keep the world's balance honest: "Kindness doesn't need permission."

The words followed her like a low lantern on a dark stretch. She did not quicken her pace. She did not slow it. Somewhere, beyond the hills, a river remembered how to be a door.

The Road That Listens

The road north left Brinvale like a frayed ribbon—mud at its edges, puddles catching the last reflections of the day. Cheri walked until the voices of the market fell behind her and only the river kept company, whispering over stones polished by a thousand small faiths.

She carried Joe's half-burned journal close against her ribs. The leather was cold, but the words inside felt alive; they pulsed faintly when her fingers brushed the cover, like a heartbeat long separated from its body. He remembered mercy when others mocked it, she thought. He wrote as if kindness were a language the world had forgotten.

Wind came down from the hills smelling of smoke—old, dry, and strangely clean. When she turned toward it, she saw what might have been a campfire flicker behind the stand of birches. The light was steady, not hungry like wild flame.

She approached quietly.

An older woman knelt beside the fire, feeding it with twigs that glowed blue at their tips. Her cloak was simple gray, the hem dark with travel. Hair escaped her braid in silver threads that caught the firelight and refused to let go. When she looked up, her eyes reflected the same quiet burn as the coals.

"Evening," Cheri said, hesitating at the ring of warmth. "I didn't mean to intrude."

The woman smiled as though the word intrude had lost its meaning long ago. "No one intrudes on a road meant to be shared." She gestured to the opposite side of the fire. "Sit. The night cools fast here."

Cheri lowered herself to the moss. They sat without speaking while the fire hummed. A kettle balanced on a flat stone began to sing softly. The stranger poured them each a cup of pale tea that smelled faintly of cedar and honey.

"You've come a long way," the woman said at last. "Farther than your shoes expected."

Cheri laughed under her breath. "You can tell that from my shoes?"

"I can tell from your eyes," the woman replied, unbothered by mystery. "They still look backward every few breaths. The heart does not like to walk faster than memory."

A House Divided by Worry

Cheri stared into the steam curling between them. "I left people who don't believe in what I'm doing. Maybe they're right."

"Maybe," the woman allowed, "and maybe the world has simply forgotten what belief looks like when it isn't afraid."

Silence again, full but not heavy. The fire popped; a spark drifted up and went out like a small blessing.

The woman reached into the worn satchel at her side and drew out a book, its binding cracked, its corners singed as if rescued from flame. "I think this belongs with what you already carry."

Cheri's breath caught. "How did you—?"

"I was near the temple after the fire," the woman said simply. "There was so much ash, but this… this still breathed. Words don't burn as easily as walls." She handed the book across the fire. "It's the rest of what he wrote."

Cheri turned the volume over in her hands. The texture matched the one she already kept, the edges of both scarred in almost the same pattern, like halves of a memory stitched by heat. When she pressed them together, the lines met perfectly.

"Who was he to you?" Cheri asked.

The woman's smile softened—wistful, proud, unbearably gentle. "A student, perhaps. Or a teacher. It's difficult to tell with souls like his. He remembered mercy when others forgot where to find it. Even after the pain, even when he believed himself cursed."

"You knew him." Cheri's voice trembled.

"I knew what he was becoming." She looked into the fire. "Every kindness he offered was an answer to a question the world had stopped asking."

Cheri swallowed hard. "The temple says he destroyed it."

"The temple would rather burn than admit it was wrong." The woman's tone was not bitter—only tired. "But you already know that. Why else would you walk this far?"

Cheri traced the journal's edge. "I think… he wrote these because the dawn spoke through him."

The woman nodded once. "Then the dawn chose well."

♥ ✳ ♥ ✳ ♥

The Fire That Speaks Her Name

For a long moment they only listened—the river murmuring beyond the trees, the wind moving through tall grass like a slow exhale. The stranger's eyes shimmered faintly, silver deepening to starlight.

"If you keep walking north," she said, "you'll find where mercy waits to be reminded of itself. When you do, tell him this: he was never alone in remembering."

Cheri looked up sharply. "You talk as if you know where he is."

But the woman had already stood. She gathered her cloak, light pooled at her feet, and when the next gust of wind came through the birches, it scattered the fire's smoke between them.

Cheri rose, coughing softly, and the clearing was empty. Only the two journals rested in her hands, edges meeting like joined wings.

She whispered into the quiet, "I'll find him. I'll remind him."

A warmth answered from the pages—soft, certain. And far away, beyond rivers and ruins, a man dreaming by another fire stirred as though someone had just spoken his name.

The wind lifted, scattering a ring of embers between them.

As Tess's outline wavered and thinned into smoke, Cheri looked down at the two journals resting open in her lap — the one she had carried from Brinvale and the one Tess had just placed into her hands. Their edges touched, almost shyly, as though the books themselves recognized each other.

A tremor passed through the leather. Ash drifted upward in tiny spirals, and a single line of silver light traced the torn seam where they met. The glow pulsed once, twice, then began to stitch its way down the spine in a slow, deliberate motion — as if time itself were sewing the wound closed.

The fire gave a soft sigh. When the light faded, the two halves had become one. The pages still bore the scorch marks of what they had endured, but now the burns curved together like joined hands.

Cheri brushed her thumb across the new seam. Warmth lingered there — faint but alive — and in it she almost heard a voice, quiet and sure as breath: He remembered, even when memory was taken.

Her throat tightened. "Then I'll remember for him," she whispered.

The wind gentled. The final curl of smoke carried Tess's scent — cedar, rain, and something older than either. The journal's spine gleamed faintly, then cooled to a soft gray, its last shimmer settling against Cheri's palm like a pulse returning home.

She pressed the mended book to her chest. The fire dimmed, but its warmth remained, as though some fragment of Tess still kept watch from the other side of the dark.

The Path North Opens

Dawn did not so much rise as breathe.
A thin veil of mist curled above the river, and dew clung to Cheri's lashes when she opened her eyes. The fire had long gone out, but the ashes were still warm,

faintly shimmering as though some unseen hand had stirred them in the night.

Beside her lay the journal — whole now, its cover cool but thrumming with a pulse she could feel through her fingertips. When she lifted it, the seam shimmered once more, then settled into stillness. It felt heavier, not with weight, but with purpose.

She sat for a while, tracing the symbols burned into the front — the remnants of smoke-blackened lines that looked almost like a heart, almost like flame. Fire that heals, Tess's voice whispered from memory, though Tess herself was gone.

Cheri turned to the first page. The handwriting was careful, deliberate. Joe's voice lived in every line — the wondering of a man caught between devotion and doubt. He wrote of mercy as strength, of faith as something more than rules. Between passages, ink had blurred where a tear or rain had fallen. She brushed the pages gently, as though comforting the memory of the one who wrote them.

When she finally closed the book, she understood.
This was not a map, but a mirror.
And she could no longer stay still.

The forest stirred awake around her — wings, rustles, distant song. She rose, slinging her pack over her shoulder. The mended journal she bound in cloth and tucked against her heart.

At the river's edge she knelt, cupping water into her hands. The surface quivered — and for a moment, her reflection blurred. Another image shimmered over it: a face she did not know but somehow recognized, eyes shadowed with guilt, the faint scar of flame over his heart.

Her breath caught. She whispered to the vision, "You are not the Destroyer. You are the dawn."

The image flickered, then dissolved. But in that instant, miles away, Joe stirred from uneasy sleep beneath a half-collapsed inn, hand clutching at the burn over his chest. For the briefest heartbeat, warmth — not pain — answered him.

Cheri rose, the hem of her cloak dark with river water.

The wind shifted north, carrying the scent of rain and distance. She took her first step onto the road, and though she walked alone, the world no longer felt silent.

With every footfall, the mist seemed to lift.
With every breath, her resolve grew.

Somewhere ahead waited the man the world called Destroyer.
She would find him.
She would call him by his true name.

And far above the waking forest, the sun broke fully over the trees — not blinding, but soft, a light that remembered how to heal.

Chapter Nine — The Test of Mercy

"Power proves nothing until it chooses restraint."

Dawn That Refuses to Be Forgotten

The dream did not end so much as thin. It left a warmth under Joe's ribs and the impression of water settling back into its banks. He opened his eyes to a roof that was more memory than shelter—rafters furred with moss, a missing slat that admitted a square of pale, rinsed dawn. Dew clung to the splinters like a faithful audience that refused to go home.

He lay still and listened to the room breathe. Old wood exhaled the night; a bird tried a note it wasn't quite sure belonged to morning. Somewhere below, the wind worked at the inn's broken door and got the same answer it had gotten yesterday: later.

His hand had already moved before his thoughts caught up. Fingers pressed the burn beneath his shirt—a scar that had stopped being a wound but hadn't decided what it was instead. Once it had been fire and panic; now it was heat remembered. Under his palm it felt less like the temple's brand and more like something the body had chosen to keep. Flame-shaped, yes. But the edges had softened, as if the skin had begun to learn a new outline and liked the lesson.

In the dream, river light had carried a face to him—a girl's, unfamiliar and known, the kind of knowing that arrives before names. Not pity in her eyes, not worship—recognition, stubborn and kind. Her mouth had shaped words, and even now the echo of them made the room feel bigger: You are not the Destroyer. You are the dawn.

He shut his eyes a moment, not to keep the dream, but to test what remained when it was gone. The heat under his palm held. A scent he had learned to associate with mercy rather than danger—cedar damp from rain—threaded the air so faintly he couldn't be certain it wasn't only memory.

"Just a dream," he said, but the dust didn't believe him, and the dust had seen him through more honest mornings than most men had.

He sat up slowly. The ache of yesterday lived in the hinges of his shoulders. He pulled on his cloak, careful not to snag the lining against the splintered sill, and tucked his shirt higher at the throat so the scar wouldn't catch an eye it didn't need. The lantern that had once kept him steady—ordinary iron and glass, not the temple's idea of holiness—rested where he'd left it beside the cold hearth. He turned the cap; the wick lifted its blackened head; the small flame consented to be, a single patient circle of light. He let it burn, then pinched it out and chose flint for the day's work, not fire born from himself. Restraint felt like a language worth practicing.

Outside, the inn's yard remembered being a yard. Weeds had taken up residence like crowded tenants and learned to share. An old sign creaked, the paint mostly gone except for a curved line that might once have promised pies or mercy. The crossroad beyond it forked toward the barley country and toward hills that had exhausted themselves into stone. He studied both and found no voice calling his name. No priest to order his steps. No boy to imitate. Just earth and a path.

He walked anyway. One step at a time, the way a man leaves a house that has done him no harm but will not help him decide the rest of his life.

The Road That Teaches Restraint

Mist held the trees at the waist; spiders had written their luminous books and signed them with dew. The air carried last night's rain and the promise of something cooking far off, the kind of bread smell that makes a road feel honest about why it exists. He let his breath take the shape of the morning rather than his fear.

Fear was still there, of course. Not the kind that makes you run from wolves—that you can see coming and decide. The other kind. The kind that walks beside you and uses your own stride to prove its point. You are dangerous. You will burn what you touch. You are an altar to the arithmetic Maldrin taught you. He answered it the only way he could manage: with smaller thoughts that didn't try to win, only to last. Light is for sight. Heat is for hands. Mercy is not a mistake.

He reached the stream that served the inn and knelt where the bank offered itself. The water went about its business, unconcerned with theologies. He cupped his hands into it and drank. Cold moved through him like a bell finding its note. He did what he had avoided since the temple fell: he looked down into the water and allowed it to hold his face. A man looked back—a little older than the boy he remembered, a little younger than the shame he carried. The burn's outline, just visible above his open collar, reflected there as a dark petal of healed skin. Not a sigil, not anymore. Not a heart, not yet. Something between— like scripture on the day before a child learns to read.

"Dawn," he tried in the low voice men reserve for truths that embarrass them. The water didn't argue. A fish flicked a fin and corrected nothing.

Memory rose without asking permission. Not the temple's version pitched from a dais; the quieter one, the one that smelled like beeswax and old stone, like someone had brought bread to a conversation and expected no applause. Tess's hands, not touching him but steadying the air around a fear until it could stand without assistance; her way of refusing to make pain into pedagogy; the sentence she had given him once when he thought he was only a container waiting to be measured: You are not a cistern, little one. You are a river. Rivers do not hoard. He couldn't put her face together from his mind's pieces the way he wanted. It came as silvery light, as the relief you feel when a fever breaks. He closed his eyes and let even that be enough.

When he opened them, he found he had been rubbing the scar without thinking. He stilled his hand and dried his fingers on his cloak. The road waited, patient. He stood and followed it.

If power wanted to announce itself that morning, it was content to do so by refusing to be necessary. Twice he felt the prickle at his wrists that always came before light gathered, and twice he did not call it. Once to move a fallen branch—a simple thing that any man with a back and breath could manage, and ought to. Once when the ground sloped toward a gulch and the wet stones would have yielded to the heat beneath his skin. He chose instead to plant his boots and test each foothold, and when the mud did slip, it sent him to a knee like an apology rather than a trial.

He took it as a lesson a child could understand without being harmed.

The road narrowed and remembered to be a path. Birds held meetings he wasn't invited to. Far off, a hammer struck iron in a rhythm that suggested order without cruelty. He found himself humming, then stopping; the tune had a temple shape and he didn't like music that made his shoulders tense. He tried again and found a melody with less furniture in it. He let it keep him company.

By midday the mist had gone to be water somewhere else. Sun filtered through birch and ash, sketching blessings on the path without needing any man to agree to them. He came to a gap where old floodwater had eaten at the bank and left the road mean and narrow. Tracks told him he was not the first to curse the washout. Wagon ruts ran to the edge and stopped in a confusion of churned mud; hoofprints overlapped the ghost of last week's rain, an ugly argument the earth had not yet had time to forget. The next stretch of safer ground lay only a stone's throw away, but the in-between made throwing unwise.

He crouched and set his palm to the dirt because that had always been a better prayer for him than most words. Under his hand the world kept humming its same low song, the one that had comforted him as a child when other boys had memorized the proper responses. It had grown quieter since the binding, yes; and even now, with the seal gone, it did not rush back like a prodigal trying to impress. It simply offered what it had, and what it had was not nothing.

He closed his eyes. He could lift a span of earth if he wanted. Not a bridge—that would be arrogance—but a firming of the soil, a small kindness to hold his weight and the weight of whatever came behind him. He felt the strength gather where strength always gathered. It was not wild; it did not paw the ground. It asked what he meant to do and promised to do only that.

His eyes stayed shut. The temple's lessons arrived wearing their best clothes and carrying their calling cards: Withhold, lest gratitude become habit. Restrain, lest love forget its leash. Portion grace, lest the unworthy learn to expect it. Behind them, quieter but nearer, came the other voice with its relentless simplicity, the one he recognized as his own even when it spoke with a cadence learned from a woman he could not name: If a thing can be made kinder, make it so.

Joe opened his eyes and removed his hand from the dirt.

"If I do this," he said to no one, to the ravine, to the morning, "let it be because I love, not because I am afraid to walk around."

He stood, waded to his shins through the least treacherous of the muck, and gained the far side with nothing worse than a soaked boot and the feeling that some small, important muscle in his mind had chosen moderation over display. He turned back and studied the ruts. They would dry on their own. Or someone with a shovel would make them honest. Not every problem was waiting for him to be a miracle and most didn't want him to be.

Mercy Tested by Fear

On the other side, the path rose into scrub and a stand of young pines that smelled clean enough to pass for certainty. He stopped and looked up. Through the needles, the sky had resumed its old work of being enormous without being cruel. Birds rode it the way children ride good shoulders.

"I am not a cistern," he said aloud, because he had to practice sentences as if they were steps. "I am not a fire for fear. I am a river, and today I will be small on purpose."

He hadn't intended it, but he smiled. It felt like a door that had been stuck and finally decided to be polite.

He started forward again, slower than he might have yesterday, and only then did he hear what the morning had been protecting from him until he was ready: up ahead, around the curve where the pines thickened and the ravine returned to test the road, voices—men's voices, clerk-sharp and hungry, cutting through a higher, frightened sound. Metal rang once, twice. A child's cry tried to be brave and failed.

Joe's hand found his chest. The scar answered, warm but not commanding. He drew one breath, then another, and did not call the light. Not yet.

He went toward the sound.

The sound found him first—metal on wood, then a voice breaking into a frightened cry. He moved without plan, half-crouched through the pines until the path opened into a clearing cut by the same road he'd been following.

A wagon sat crooked in the mud. Three men worked at its sides like termites. One tugged at the harness of a horse too thin for labor; another ripped open a grain sack; the third held a knife toward a woman who kept her body between the blade and the child clinging to her skirt.

Joe stepped from the trees. The light that lived in him stirred as though it had been waiting for permission. He closed his hand around the feeling and spoke first.

"Leave her."

The knife man turned, mouth bent in something between a grin and a snarl. "Leave her, he says." He looked Joe over, taking in the cloak, the travel dirt, the absence of badge or weapon. "You alone, preacher?"

"Alone enough."

The words tasted strange—half prayer, half promise.

The bandit lunged. Joe's hand came up without thought, palm open, and a flare leapt from it like sunlight breaking through storm. The air snapped; the blade flew from the man's grip and landed ten paces away, hissing in the mud. The horse screamed but did not fall.

For a heartbeat, silence had edges. Then smoke rose from the ground between them, a narrow black scar in the soil. Joe's mark burned in reply, heat threading through his chest, but this time the fire did not demand more.

"Go," he said.

They went. Even thieves knew when the road changed owners.

The woman knelt beside the wheel, whispering thanks that spilled into sobs. "Mercy on you," she said, reaching toward his sleeve. "Mercy for sending—"

"Don't," Joe said, stepping back. "Just take your child and go."

She obeyed, half dragging the boy, half carrying him, the sound of their retreat swallowed by the trees. When they were gone, the smell of burnt cedar lingered like a question that refused to be graded.

He sank to one knee, pressing his hand over the scar. It pulsed once, steady, and eased. No ruin, no uncontrolled blaze—only warmth. For the first time since the temple fell, he didn't flinch from it.

"Mercy," he whispered, as if naming an animal he hoped would stay tame.

Far away, on a road washed clean by dawn, Cheri's pack shifted against her shoulder. The journal inside grew warm enough that she stopped walking. She opened it to a page she hadn't yet reached. A new line had written itself in ink pale as dawnfire:

Mercy need not raise its voice to be heard.

She touched the words with her fingertips. Somewhere she didn't know, a man was learning the same lesson the hard way, and the world had quietly taken note.

Joe stood, breathing smoke and pine and fear and relief all at once. He turned toward the north. The scar beneath his shirt cooled to the rhythm of his heartbeat, as if it too had decided that surviving could count as faith for one more day.

The Cost of a Kindness

Twilight bled into the edges of the forest, a slow spill of gold turned rust. Joe stayed by the road long after the woman's wagon disappeared, the hush of her gratitude lingering heavier than any threat. The smell of scorched cedar refused to fade. It wound through the air, clean but unshakable—a reminder that even mercy left marks.

He sat at the edge of the ruts, boots buried in mud that was already cooling, and let his hands rest open on his knees. The ache behind his ribs was familiar—the place where faith tried to rebuild itself after collapse.

"I didn't mean to," he said quietly, though no one accused him. "I only wanted to stop the harm."

The world did not answer, but it listened.

Above him, crows traced a slow circle against the red-gold horizon. Somewhere to the east, a bell rang from a chapel that had been long abandoned; the sound carried faint and directionless through the trees. He tilted his head toward it like a man remembering a hymn.

If this was mercy, it wasn't the kind the temple praised. It didn't demand witnesses. It didn't burn brighter for being seen. It simply was.

Joe rose, stretching the ache from his back, and turned toward the river's whisper far below the slope. He followed it through the trees until the light pooled silver across its surface. The scar under his shirt warmed as though recognizing the sound.

♥ ✳ ♥ ✳ ♥

Where Rivers Remember Names

Kneeling, he reached out and let his fingertips break the reflection. The ripples ran outward and kept running, crossing leagues of water and faith until they brushed against another set of fingers—Cheri's— where she knelt at a distant bend, the same current catching her hair like a halo of dusk.

Neither saw the other. Both felt the pull.

Joe's breath caught; a whisper slipped through the reeds—too soft for language, but bright enough for recognition. He knew that voice, though he could not name it. He thought it must be a dream, a mercy hallucinated by guilt. Yet in that instant, he felt something like prayer answer prayer: her warmth meeting his shadow.

He drew back sharply, staring at his reflection until it blurred. "No," he muttered. "Stay away. I'll ruin you, too."

The river said nothing, but its surface shivered once, like laughter disguised as wind.

Joe rose and stepped back, heart pounding. He pulled his cloak tight around him, hiding the faint ember-glow through the fabric. If the world wanted a destroyer, he would give them silence instead.

He left the river behind, following the road north. The lantern at his belt knocked softly against his hip—an ordinary sound, grounding him. Yet for one heartbeat before he vanished into the trees, the flame-shaped scar over his heart pulsed with quiet light.

And miles away, Cheri's journal answered—its pages trembling as if to say: Found you.

Chapter Ten — The Road Between

"Out of the ash the river remembered its course, and I followed

its heart."

Ash on the Road North

The valley had not yet decided whether it was alive.

Smoke still hung low, clinging to the hollows where trees had stood before the firestorm. The air smelled of salt and char, the scent of things half-healed, half-gone. Wind moved strangely now—slow and careful, as though the world feared that breathing too deep might reopen its wounds.

Cheri walked alone beside the river, tracing its slow return to life. The current was thin and gray where ash still drifted, but now and then the water caught a shard of sunlight and gleamed clear. Each flash felt like a heartbeat under her ribs. She followed that rhythm because there was nothing else to follow.

No roads survived this far north—only ridges of scorched earth and the faint sound of moving water. She had prayed for direction and received silence, prayed again and received ache. That ache, low and insistent, had drawn her onward like the echo of a name she could not quite recall.

Her boots left shallow prints in soot-soft soil. When she paused to rest, the river spoke in low ripples that sounded almost like words. Somewhere beyond the haze, a hawk cried once and was gone.

She thought of the stories—the ones told in whispers after the Temple fell. A destroyer walking north, they said. A man of light and ruin. Every rumor pointed toward death. Yet her pendant glowed whenever she prayed for him, a slow pulse like breath through glass. It had begun the night she saw the sky burn.

She pressed her palm to the small crystal at her throat.

"Guide me," she whispered. "If he still lives, let mercy find him before judgment does."

The light beneath her hand brightened, then steadied.
So she kept walking.

By mid-day she reached the lower bend where the river widened into a pale mirror. The wind shifted, carrying the faint iron tang of blood. She froze. A shape moved near the water's edge—tall, broad-shouldered, head bowed. He knelt among several still forms laid carefully in a half-circle, each with hands folded and eyes closed. The earth around them had been washed clean.

Cheri crept closer, her heart beating faster than sense allowed.
The man's coat was torn and stained; ash streaked his hair and beard. Yet there was reverence in his movements, a gentleness that seemed foreign in this ruined place. He placed a stone at one body's feet, whispered something she couldn't hear, then touched his chest as if in benediction.

A faint glow answered beneath his collar. It wasn't the cruel blaze the temple had feared—it was a muted pulse, as if light itself mourned.

Her breath caught. It's him.

The name she'd carried in prayer pressed hard behind her lips, but she dared not speak it. Instead she watched as he knelt again, shoulders trembling, hands shaking over another fallen traveler. The light flickered and dimmed.

Without thinking, she stepped forward. Pebbles shifted under her boot, the small sound cutting through the hush. The man turned sharply, his eyes catching the riverlight.

For an instant the world narrowed to that gaze. Those eyes were haunted—gray shot with pale gold, the color of storm clouds remembering dawn. They carried exhaustion deeper than wounds, yet when he looked at her, something softened.

He rose slowly, as if uncertain she was real. The faint glow beneath his collar steadied once more.

The pendant at her throat pulsed in perfect time with it.

Between them, the river shimmered with the same rhythm—ash drifting on the surface like forgotten prayers.

Cheri's lips parted, but no words came. The ache beneath her ribs was gone now, replaced by quiet knowing. She didn't need a map, or a prophecy, or even courage. She only needed to cross the water.

The Dead Who Needed Naming

The water was colder than she expected.
It lapped around her boots, tugging at the hem of her cloak as if the river itself wished to slow her. She ignored it, stepping carefully from stone to stone until she reached the other side. The man—Joe, though she had not yet spoken the name—watched in wary silence.

When she drew near, he stepped back a pace, shoulders tensing as if her presence carried danger.

Joe: "You shouldn't come closer. The dead don't need more witnesses."

Cheri: "Maybe not. But the living do."

Her voice was quiet, steady in the way water is steady even when it moves. He looked away first, toward the makeshift graves, then down at his hands. They were raw and shaking, smeared with soot.

Joe: "I tried to help them. It— it keeps coming out wrong."

Cheri: "You helped them remember they were human."

She knelt beside one of the fallen. Someone had placed a small token—an old copper pendant—on the woman's folded hands. Cheri touched it lightly. The copper was still warm.

Cheri: "You gave them peace, Joe."

He flinched at the sound of his name, as though struck.

Joe: "Don't call me that."
Cheri: "Why not?"
Joe: "Because it belongs to someone who should've died back there."

The wind shifted, carrying the scent of river reeds and rain beginning to fall. For a long moment neither spoke. Cheri turned to him slowly, studying the man she had prayed for. The stories called him destroyer; the temple had branded him cursed. Yet here he stood, mourning strangers.

She reached toward him, stopping just short of touch.

Cheri: "Then let me call you what you are now."
Joe (bitterly): "And what's that?"
Cheri: "Heart of the Dawn."

He laughed once, harsh and small. "That's a story, not a man."

Cheri's eyes softened. "Every story begins with someone who forgot he was one."

Rain began to fall in earnest, small droplets hissing against the ash. Joe's light pulsed again beneath his collar, bright enough now to spill through the fabric. He winced and clutched his chest.

Cheri moved closer.

Cheri: "Let me see."

He shook his head, but the pain bent him to one knee. When he did not resist further, she eased his tunic open.

The mark beneath was worse than she'd imagined: a blackened sigil, burned deep into his flesh, edges still faintly glowing. Light flickered through cracks like embers trapped under skin. It was beautiful in the way lightning is beautiful—terrible because it hurts to look at.

Cheri reached out, fingers trembling.

♥ ✳ ♥ ✳ ♥

Where Wounds Remember Light

Joe: "It won't stop. It never stops."
Cheri: "That's because it was never meant to be sealed."

She laid her palm over the mark.
The pendant at her throat flared; the light under his skin brightened in answer. Between their hands, warmth surged—not heat, but the steady warmth of sunrise after frost. Joe gasped, muscles locking as the black lines softened to red, then gold. The scar's shape shifted slowly, curling into a pattern that resembled a heart framed in dawnfire.

The rain stilled.

When the light faded, her palm still rested against his chest. Beneath it, his heartbeat felt strong— stronger than her own.

Cheri (whispering): "There. You see? It was never a curse."
Joe: "Then what is it?"
Cheri: "A promise."

He exhaled, long and shuddering, and for the first time since the Temple's fall, tears broke loose. They mingled with the rain and washed the soot from his face. Cheri did not look away. She only lowered her hand, leaving a faint golden shimmer where her touch had been.

Joe: "Why would you do that for me?"
Cheri: "Because mercy doesn't keep score."

The sound of the river changed then—no longer a dirge but a low, living song. Even the clouds thinned enough for a pale band of light to fall across them both.

By nightfall the rain had passed.
Mist clung to the low ground, curling around the trunks of half-burned trees. Cheri gathered driftwood from the riverbank while Joe stacked stones into a

small ring. When he struck flint to steel, the spark caught on the first try. The flame rose thin and unsteady before finding its rhythm — a heartbeat echoing the one newly healed beneath his chest.

They sat opposite each other, the fire between them.
For a long time neither spoke. The only sound was the crackle of damp wood and the distant murmur of the river, gentler now than it had been that morning.

Cheri unfastened her cloak and spread it across the ground.

Cheri: "You should rest. You've carried the dead all day."

Joe: "I'm fine."

Cheri: "You're not."

He looked up sharply, ready to argue, but stopped when he saw her expression. It wasn't pity. It was understanding — a calm that didn't deny the pain, only made space for it.

Joe (quietly): "I don't know how to stop feeling responsible."

Cheri: "Maybe you don't stop. Maybe you let it become something else."

She drew a small leather book from her satchel — worn, edges darkened with age. He stared at it, confused.

Joe: "That looks like mine."

Cheri: "It was found among the ashes. I thought you might want it back."

He reached out, hesitated, then took it. The leather was cracked but still warm, as if it remembered him. He opened to the first page, eyes tracing cramped script — notes on faith, fragments of prayers, sketches of the Heartline symbol half-burned by fire.

A Fire That Does Not Burn

Joe: "I used to write about light as if it were a person."

Cheri: "Maybe it still is."

Joe: "Someone taught me that once."

Cheri: "Who?"

Joe (after a pause): "I … don't remember. Only her voice — soft, certain. Like she believed I could be more than I was."

Cheri's smile was gentle.

Cheri: "Then keep listening. Sometimes faith returns before the memory does."

The fire popped, sending sparks spiraling upward. Joe turned another page. Some lines were lost to flame, yet others endured — small miracles of ink and stubborn hope. He brushed his thumb over one surviving line.

Joe (reading): " 'Mercy isn't the absence of judgment; it's the refusal to end the story there.' "

Cheri: "Do you believe that now?"

Joe: "I want to."

Cheri: "That's a start."

Silence settled again, this time companionable.
He closed the journal and tried to hand it back.

Joe: "You keep it. You read it better than I do."

Cheri: "No. It belongs with you. Maybe it can remind
you who you're becoming."

He tucked it into his coat without protest. The
motion looked like acceptance, or at least the
beginning of it.

Cheri: "Tomorrow we'll head south. There's a
village rebuilding near the marshes. They could use
both of us."

Joe (half-smile): "You always speak as if the world's
waiting for permission to heal."

Cheri: "It is. It just needs someone to say the first 'yes.'
"

When the fire burned low, they lay a few paces
apart — her cloak spread between them, the journal

beneath his arm. Above them, the stars had begun to return, faint at first, then brighter, one by one.

Cheri watched until her eyes grew heavy. Just before sleep claimed her, she felt warmth brush her skin — not the fire, but something deeper, as though the light itself leaned close to listen.

Dawn came gently, a gray blush sliding across the river.
Mist lifted in pale threads from the water, winding between the trees like smoke that had forgotten why it burned. The fire had died to coals, but the air still held its warmth.

Cheri woke first.
For a while she only lay still, listening — the river breathing, the soft rasp of Joe's steady sleep on the other side of the embers. He looked younger in the morning light, the hard lines of guilt softened by rest. A stray lock of hair had fallen over his brow. It made him look almost peaceful, almost ordinary.

She wanted to believe he could stay that way.

The healed mark beneath his collar faintly glimmered, the slow pulse of dawnfire beneath skin. Each heartbeat sent a thread of light along the veins of his chest before it faded again. It wasn't blinding now; it was beautiful — a quiet reminder that mercy had left its signature where shame once lived.

Cheri drew her knees up and hugged them close. The pendant at her throat — now dim and content — warmed against her skin.

He's free, she thought. He just doesn't know what to do with freedom yet.

A heron called upriver, the sound long and hollow. Joe stirred, eyes blinking open to the dim light.

Joe (hoarse): "You're awake early."
Cheri (smiling): "Someone had to make sure the world was still here."
Joe: "And is it?"
Cheri: "For now."

♥ ✳ ♥ ✳ ♥

Dawn That Demands Choosing

He sat up, rubbing his face with both hands. When he looked at her, something unspoken passed between them — gratitude, maybe, or the beginning of understanding.

Joe: "You should keep the journal after all. I think I'd just fill it with apologies."
Cheri: "Then start with one to yourself. That's where forgiveness begins."

He didn't answer, but his half-smile said she was right. They shared a small breakfast — bread dried from her pack and river water that tasted faintly of ash. The simplicity of it felt sacred.

When they finished, he rose and began tying his cloak, movements brisk and deliberate.

Cheri: "You're leaving?"
Joe: "There's a ridge east of here. Villages beyond it might need help."

Cheri: "So will the ones south of here."

Joe (quiet): "Then maybe mercy will split its path."

He reached for his pack, hesitated, then turned back.

Joe: "Thank you… for reminding me I'm not the destroyer."

Cheri: "You never were."

He looked at her a long time, as if trying to memorize something he couldn't name.

Joe: "If the light still has work for me, I'll follow it."

Cheri: "Then so will I."

Their eyes met; the world seemed to hold still. Sunlight crested the ridge then, touching the healed mark on his chest until it shone like living gold. The reflection danced across the river and lit her pendant in reply — two pulses answering one another.

Cheri (softly): "Dawnfire suits you."

Joe (a faint grin): "And you? What should the light call

you?”

Cheri: “Faithheart.”

He nodded once — an acknowledgment, a promise, and something like farewell.
Then he turned toward the east, walking until the mist swallowed him.

Cheri watched until the last trace of his silhouette dissolved into light. The ache in her chest was familiar now, but no longer painful. It was hope, learning how to breathe.

She whispered to the quiet morning:

“Go where mercy leads, Dawnfire. I’ll find you when it’s time.”

The river caught her words and carried them onward, its surface glimmering gold in the first full light of day.

Chapter Eleven – Faithheart's Return

"Mercy travels faster than rumor; faith travels slower, but it never loses the road."

The Return Home

The southern road was less a path than a scar. Ash still powdered the ditches, and when Cheri's boots pressed into it, faint wisps rose like the ghosts of seeds that had never sprouted. Yet beneath that gray crust, life waited. Each footprint released the smell of damp soil, of roots remembering rain.

She kept the river to her left. It was her compass and her confession both. Every time it curved toward her, the pendant at her throat brightened as if the current itself approved of her direction. She whispered prayers without words—thank-yous, promises, fragments of gratitude that needed no language.

Mid-morning found her crossing the ruins of a hamlet burned clean to its foundations. The stones were still black, but from the cracks between them green shoots had begun to climb, defiant as laughter in a funeral hall. She stooped and touched one—tiny, delicate, absurdly alive.

Cheri (softly): "You remember how to rise."

Behind her, someone cleared his throat. A boy stood there, maybe twelve, a shovel slung across one shoulder. His eyes flicked from her pendant to the sprout she cradled.

Boy: "Are you the light-woman? The one they say walks with the fire-man?"
Cheri (smiling): "No one walks with fire. They walk after it, and plant again."
Boy: "Mama says he burned the world."
Cheri: "Maybe he did. But fire doesn't choose what it burns. Mercy chooses what it saves."

The boy frowned, considering that, then nodded once and trudged back toward a row of broken chimneys. Cheri watched him go, heart tight with tenderness. The story was already changing. Rumor had outrun truth, but mercy was catching up.

By noon, the land softened. Meadows replaced stone; the grass grew thin but green. Insects hummed—a sound she hadn't heard in months. She stopped at a shallow stream to drink. When she leaned close, her reflection shimmered over the water: dirt-streaked face, hair tangled, eyes steady. Behind the exhaustion she saw something else—light returning, slow but sure.

She touched the pendant. The runes beneath her sleeve responded, pulsing once. The faint warmth traveled up her arm and into her chest. It wasn't power exactly—it was connection, the quiet knowledge that somewhere beyond the horizon, he still breathed.

You're alive. And learning to heal without me.

The thought ached, but in the best way.

She reached the next village before dusk. A handful of homes stood half-rebuilt around a central square. Smoke rose from hearths that smelled of bread instead of burning. When the people noticed her pendant's dim light, they drew close—not afraid, only curious.

Elder Woman: "You come from the north?"
Cheri: "From the ashlands."
Man: "Did you see him?"
Cheri: "Who?"
Man: "The one they call Dawnfire. Some say he brings storms; others, rain."

Cheri hesitated, choosing her words carefully.

Cheri: "He brings what the heart is ready for."

A murmur rippled through them. A child tugged at her sleeve, eyes wide.

Child: "Is he real?"
Cheri (kneeling): "He was lost. Now he's found. The finding makes him real."

The villagers offered her food and a corner of their fire that night. As they ate, she told small stories—not sermons, only moments. How a field had turned green again where he knelt. How kindness had lit a wound. How mercy could take the shape of an ordinary man.

They listened the way dry soil drinks water.

Later, when the camp quieted, she slipped away to the edge of the square and watched the stars rise. They were clearer here, as though distance itself had been washed. For the first time she realized she could trace the Heartline constellation—a curved arc of silver light sweeping across the sky.

Her pendant pulsed once in rhythm with it.

Cheri (to herself): "You see it too, don't you?"

The breeze answered with the scent of lilac from some half-blooming shrub. She smiled, wrapping her cloak tighter. Tomorrow she would continue south, back to her own village—the place she'd left with faith but no certainty. Now she carried both.

The road shimmered faintly ahead, lit by moonlight and memory. She whispered a small prayer for strength, then stepped forward. The earth, newly softened by rain, held her footprints a little longer this time before letting them go.

By the second evening, the road began to feel familiar.
The marshland air grew heavier, smelling of wild mint and river clay, and the sky bent low over the hills as if the world were holding its breath for her return.
She walked slower now. Not because she was tired, but because every step pressed closer to memory — the place she had left when obedience to a dream seemed easier than explaining it.

Ahead, lanterns flickered along the rise that marked the edge of her home village. The lights shimmered through the mist like a handful of stars fallen too near the ground. Somewhere behind them, Patty's cottage would be waiting, tilted and warm, smoke curling like a lazy thought from the chimney.
Cheri smiled at the picture in her mind. Patty will scold

me first, then feed me twice over. Some miracles never change.

But before she could go to the woman who had been more mother than the one who bore her, Cheri turned up the stone path toward the house on the hill. Old shadows needed facing.

The House on the Hill

The door opened to the same breath of lavender and flour she remembered from childhood — precise, uninviting, clean to the point of loneliness.
Her mother stood in the doorway, hands dusted white, eyes darting to the faint glow at Cheri's throat.

Mother: "So the stories were true."
Cheri: "If you mean the ones about surviving, yes."
Mother: "About consorting with the one they called Destroyer."

Cheri met her gaze without lowering her head.

Cheri: "They call him Dawnfire now."
Mother: "Names don't change what a thing is."
Cheri: "No. But mercy does."

A silence like a drawn blade stretched between them.
Then came the smooth voice she half-expected — her brother's. He stepped from the inner room, robes perfectly pressed, expression polished to superiority.

Brother: "So our wayward sister returns. Tell me, Cheri — did mercy rebuild the Temple after you burned it down?"
Cheri: "No. It built something better."
Brother: "A myth?"
Cheri: "A chance."

Her father lingered behind them, kind eyes half-hidden by restraint. He gave a small nod — permission without defiance, love without courage.

Cheri: "I came to help, not to argue."
Mother: "Then start by cleaning the mud off your boots before it stains my floor."

Cheri bowed slightly, a motion that looked like obedience but tasted of forgiveness, and turned away. Outside, the wind met her like an old friend. The pendant at her throat warmed, a steady heartbeat reminding her she'd done what she needed to do.

Patty's Cottage

Down the slope, the square buzzed with evening voices.
Lanterns swayed over new market stalls patched together from half-burned timbers, the scent of baking bread mixing with smoke and hope.
Past the square, between two willow trees whose roots drank from the same stream, stood Patty's cottage — its walls uneven, its windows laughing with light.

Before Cheri could knock, the door swung wide. Patty stood there, hands on hips, grin wide enough to shame the sun.

Patty: "So the prodigal returns. Did the sky fall or just your stubbornness?"
Cheri (laughing): "Both, I think."

They hugged until Cheri's knees gave a little. When Patty finally stepped back, she studied her like an artifact rediscovered.

Patty: "You've changed."
Cheri: "The world made sure of it."
Patty: "Good. Sit. Tell me everything while I feed you too much."

Inside smelled of rosemary and woodsmoke, the kind of smell that made even silence feel fed.
Cheri told the story in fragments — the journey north, the people she'd met, the man who believed himself a destroyer until mercy proved him wrong.
She didn't use his name, but Patty saw it anyway in the light behind her eyes.

Patty: "So that's what you found out there. A man who needed reminding."
Cheri: "And maybe I needed reminding too."

Patty: "The world breaks us just enough to make space for light. Now eat."

They both laughed, and for the first time since she'd left, Cheri felt whole enough to be hungry.

Rumors in the Square

By dusk the next day, word had spread.
A handful of villagers drifted to Patty's fence with excuses — fresh bread, herbs, gossip carried like offerings.
Curiosity glimmered behind every smile.

Elder Woman: "Is it true, then? You're Faithheart?"
Cheri: "If that name means mercy still works, then yes."

A ripple of relief moved through the small crowd.
One young mason stepped forward, hat in hand.

Mason: "They say Dawnfire healed the river up north. Is it true?"
Cheri: "He did more than that. He remembered how."

Patty watched from the porch, arms folded, pretending to scowl.

Patty: "You've turned half the town into believers without a sermon."
Cheri: "Belief starts small — in how we treat each other."

Patty: "Then keep treating them kindly. But don't skip supper doing it."

Evening Visitors

When night fell, Janis arrived, cloak damp from travel and heart full of news.
Cheri met her at the gate, and the two women fell into each other's arms like pages finally finding their binding.

Janis: "Rumor outran you. They're calling you Faithheart and him Dawnfire."

Cheri: "Then mercy finally has names."

Janis: "Careful. The elders won't like seeing their power replaced by kindness."

Cheri: "Kindness doesn't need permission."

Patty (from the kitchen): "Or paperwork."

They all laughed until the kettle whistled.
Later, the three sat outside under the eaves as rain whispered through the herb garden.
Lantern light pooled in the puddles, each reflection trembling like a tiny dawn.

Janis: "He'll come back, you know."

Cheri: "He will. The world always leads us back to what we healed."

Patty: "And if it doesn't, you'll just go drag him home yourself."

Cheri (smiling): "Maybe I will."

Inside, long after the others slept, Cheri opened her journal.
The pendant glowed softly, lighting the page as she

wrote.

Each word felt like planting: faith, mercy, dawn.
When she closed the book, she whispered,

"The world is listening now. Let it hear love first."

Outside, wind brushed through the garden,
carrying the smell of mint and distant rain — a
promise rather than a storm.

Morning broke soft and gold, clouds the color of
cream drifting low over the marsh.
Birdsong stitched the silence together. The village
smelled of new bread and damp soil — the scent of a
world remembering how to live.

Cheri rose before Patty and stepped barefoot into
the garden. The dew chilled her feet, but the pendant
at her throat warmed, pulsing with a faint rhythm that
matched her heart. She smiled and knelt among the
mint and feverfew, pressing seedlings into the loosened
earth. Whenever her fingers brushed the soil, the
warmth deepened; tiny beads of dew steamed off the
leaves in a shimmer that looked like breath.

Patty appeared in the doorway, shawl wrapped around her shoulders.

Patty: "If you're planning to work miracles before breakfast, at least save me one."
Cheri (laughing): "These are just plants. They already know what to do."
Patty: "Most people could learn from them."

The sun lifted higher. Light filtered through the willow branches and glinted off the pendant, scattering gold across the garden walls. When the light touched Patty's face, her scowl softened into a smile she tried to hide behind her mug of tea.

The South Field

By midmorning, Janis arrived, sleeves rolled, hair tied back, carrying a basket heavy with seed grain.

Janis: "The south field's dead again. The elders say it's cursed."

Patty: "That field isn't cursed. It's just tired of being prayed over instead of planted."
Cheri: "Then let's remind it that faith works best with hands in the dirt."

The three women walked past the square to the barren patch of land beyond the mill.
The air smelled faintly of ash even after all these months. Cracks veined the ground, hard and gray. Villagers stood watching from the road — not jeering, not mocking, just waiting to see if hope still meant anything.

Cheri stepped forward first. She knelt and pressed both palms flat against the soil.

Cheri: "The land remembers mercy. It only needs to be asked kindly."

She closed her eyes. The pendant glowed softly, light seeping down her arms like warmth flowing through water. Janis scattered seeds over the furrows, steady and deliberate, while Patty covered them with soil, muttering under her breath about blisters and faith in equal measure.

A hush rippled through the air.
The cracked earth trembled once, then relaxed.
A single green shoot pushed through, small but defiant. Then another, and another, until a faint shimmer of green dusted the field like an answered prayer.

Patty (awed): "Well, look at that."
Janis: "I told you the ground just needed kindness."
Patty: "Kindness and good seed. Don't start thinking you can glow your way through every problem, Faithheart."

The crowd began to murmur, wonder replacing fear. Children ran forward to touch the shoots until their parents called them back, half-scolding, half-crying.

The Elders' Visit

That evening, when the field still glowed faintly under moonlight, three elders came to Patty's gate. Their robes were clean, their expressions polite but wary.

The eldest, Helem, spoke first.

Helem: "We hear you've been performing signs."
Cheri: "Only planting."
Elder 2: "The people call them miracles."
Patty (dryly): "People say many things when they're happy. I'd let them have it."
Helem: "Happiness without order becomes chaos."

Cheri met his eyes, calm but unyielding.

Cheri: "Then maybe order should remember joy."

A long silence followed — not defiance, but confusion from those who'd forgotten what humility felt like.

Finally Helem sighed.

Helem: "Continue your work, but do not call it holy."
Cheri: "Mercy doesn't need titles."

They left without another word. Patty barred the door and muttered,

Patty: "I liked it better when holiness stayed home and did its chores."

Rumors and Reach

Days passed. The south field thickened with green. Every stalk rose taller, fed not only by rain but by laughter. People began to help without being asked — carrying water, mending fences, baking bread for workers. It wasn't a movement yet, but it was momentum.

Travelers stopped by, bringing news of distant healings:
rivers running clear again in the north, fires that cleansed instead of burned, small villages where strangers worked together instead of hiding apart. Each story ended the same way — whispered reverently:

"Dawnfire walked here."

The first night Janis read those words aloud from a trader's letter, Cheri felt her pendant thrum softly against her chest. The warmth was unmistakable — distant but real, as if someone far away had whispered her name to the wind.
She pressed a hand over it, closed her eyes, and breathed,

"You're still out there… and you're still choosing mercy."

Patty didn't ask. She only smiled from her chair and poured another cup of tea.

Harvest and Hope

By midsummer, the south field shimmered gold under the sun.
The first harvest was modest, but it fed every household.

Cheri refused payment, asking only that each family save double the seed for the next planting and give half to anyone in need.

Cheri: "That's how mercy grows — not from preaching, but from planting."
Janis: "Then the Heart of the Dawn will never run out of soil."

People began to call them the Circle of Mercy — just neighbors helping neighbors, unaware they were founding something that would one day change the world.

Evening at the Garden

That night, after the last sheaf was stored, Cheri sat beside the garden fence with Patty and Janis.
Fireflies drifted between them like sparks from an unseen forge.
The smell of mint and bread floated on the warm air.

Patty: "So, what's next, Faithheart?"

Cheri: "We keep planting. The rest will find its way."

Patty: "And him?"

Cheri: "He's already finding his."

The pendant brightened once, soft and steady. Somewhere far to the north, another light answered. No one saw it, but they all felt the change in the air — the sense that mercy had taken root and would keep spreading, seed by seed, until even the coldest ground remembered spring.

Chapter Twelve – Echoes of Dawnfire

"Some fires do not burn to destroy.
They burn to remind the dark that light still remembers
its name."

The Barn

Snow fell in quiet flakes that hissed when they struck the blackened stones.

Joe walked through the ruin of what had once been a northern hamlet—nothing left but char and silence. Each step sank into soot, and when he looked behind him, the wind erased his footprints almost as quickly as he made them.

He had stopped counting days. The sky here kept no measure of time, only light and its absence. His coat was ragged, boots mended with thread torn from his own sleeves, yet the **scar over his heart**—the mark that once seared him with shame—no longer burned. Sometimes it warmed, faintly, when he knelt beside someone who needed help.

A collapsed barn lay ahead, smoke still whispering from the beams. Joe jogged forward, shoulders bowed against the cold. He found a man half-buried in snow, coughing ash.

Joe: "Don't move. You're still breathing. That's enough to start with."

He dragged the man free, tearing cloth from his own coat to bind a wound. When he pressed a hand to the man's chest, warmth pulsed from beneath Joe's palm—subtle, steady. The light was faint, but it flowed cleanly, carrying no fury. Only mercy.

When the man opened his eyes, Joe smiled without meaning to.

Joe: "Rest. The dawn still knows where to find us."

The villager stared, lips forming the word *"Dawnfire?"* before sleep claimed him.

Joe froze. He hadn't used that name; he hadn't spoken it aloud since Cheri.

Somewhere, rumor had outrun him.

The next village greeted him with bread and questions.

An old woman pressed his hands between hers and whispered,

Old Woman: "They say your fire leaves no scars."

Joe: "It leaves lessons."

Old Woman: "Then teach us."

He did. He showed them how to warm stone for cooking without flame, how to draw heat from the ground instead of the forest, how to sing while they worked so the rhythm carried the burden away. It wasn't magic, not as the Temple defined it. It was mercy taking form.

By evening, laughter rose over the hills like smoke that refused to stay down.

That night, Joe built a small fire alone at the edge of camp.

The scar on his chest pulsed softly, and for the first time he didn't fear it.

He held his hands near the flames and whispered into the darkness:

"You were right, Cheri. It was never about control."

The wind shifted, bringing the scent of mint and rain—her scent.

He closed his eyes, smiling through the ache of missing her.

Far away, a pulse of warmth brushed his heart, so gentle he thought he'd imagined it.

But he knew better.

Somewhere south of him, mercy had answered.

By the time the snows began to thin, the roads filled with sound again — wagons creaking, wheels slushing through meltwater, the low hum of travelers carrying news as if it were warmth.

Joe moved among them without ceremony, cloak pulled close, beard rough from weeks without rest. He looked like any other wanderer until he stopped to help. That was when people whispered.

At first it was only gratitude — a man whose fever broke after Joe's hand brushed his brow, a child whose cough eased when he lit a small fire nearby. But gratitude has a way of turning into story, and story into legend.

> **Traveler 1 (to another):** "They say the fire listens to him."
> **Traveler 2:** "They say he's looking for the woman they call Faithheart."
> **Traveler 1:** "Then mercy walks the world in pairs."

Joe never corrected them. He only smiled faintly and changed the subject to what they needed rebuilt — roofs, bridges, broken plows. His hands remembered work; his heart remembered light.

He spent a week in a fishing town at the mouth of the Serin River, where the ice still gripped the docks. The boats were frozen fast, the men idle and angry.

Joe studied the ice, then struck the wooden posts with his staff — not with power, but with rhythm.

A sound like distant thunder answered, and cracks bloomed across the surface, spreading outward in delicate veins. Within the hour, the river was free again.

Fisherman: "How'd you do that?"
Joe: "Told the river it was time to breathe."

They laughed, uncertain whether to believe him, and began pushing boats into the current. When they turned back, he was already gone, leaving only warmth where he'd stood.

That night, in taverns miles away, sailors told
the tale of *Dawnfire who freed the river*.
Each retelling added a detail — light in his hands, a
woman's voice in the wind, or a song that thawed ice.
None of them were true, yet none were false either.

The Camp of the Lost

Three days later, Joe found a camp of refugees
huddled in the skeleton of an old watchtower. They'd
fled the northern mines, coughing black dust, skin gray
from starvation. He sat among them, passing bread
until his own pack was empty.
When night fell, they gathered close to his small fire.

Refugee Girl: "Are you the Dawnfire?"
Joe (quietly): "Just someone who remembers
the dawn."
Refugee Girl: "Then tell us about it."

So he did — not as sermon, but as story. He spoke of a time when light and song had walked together; when mercy had a face and laughter carried across fields still green. He spoke of a woman who saw the world not as broken but as waiting to be healed.

When he finished, the girl was asleep, and the others sat with eyes closed as if trying to see what he saw.

Joe looked at the embers, thinking how Cheri's words had sounded that first night by the river: *You are not a destroyer, Joe. You're the heart that stayed when everything else ran away.*

The scar on his chest warmed again — gentle, steady.

He whispered into the darkness,

"I'm still listening."

Echoes

By spring, his name and Cheri's had become entwined in every market and outpost:
Faithheart and Dawnfire, the twin flames of mercy.

Some swore they traveled together; others said they were spirits who passed unseen, leaving healed ground where they walked.

Joe heard these stories as he moved from place to place, and though part of him wanted to deny them, another part knew the truth behind the rumor — mercy didn't need accuracy, only witness.

He started leaving small symbols behind — a mark shaped like a rising sun etched into wood or stone.

Not a temple's brand, just a reminder.
When the villagers asked its meaning, he said,

"It means remember light."

At night, he'd rest by the fire, staring north where stars cut the horizon sharp. Each time the flames swayed, he felt a pulse echo through the scar beneath his hand. The warmth never hurt now; it only guided.

Somewhere far away, he knew Cheri felt it too.

The northern wind came down hard from the mountains that week, dragging sleet and the smell of stone. Joe followed the road until it bent toward a valley where the smoke of hearths clung low, heavy and gray.

The place was called **Brimvale**, though no brim or vale remained — just scarred ground and a church of blackened timber. The people here still burned offerings at dusk, hoping to keep ruin away. When they saw the stranger approach, their faces turned cautious, like shutters half-closed against storm.

He raised a hand in greeting.

Joe: "Evening."

No one answered. The silence felt old.

A thin man in a priest's robe stepped forward, staff clutched like a weapon.

Priest: "Travelers don't stop here. The curse clings to strangers."
Joe: "Then maybe it's time the curse had company."

The man blinked, unsure whether to be offended or relieved.

The Sick Boy

Inside one of the cottages, a child lay fevered and still, skin too pale for breath.
The mother sat beside him, lips moving soundlessly, eyes dry from praying past tears.

Joe knelt opposite her. "May I?"
She hesitated, then nodded once.

He laid his hand over the boy's heart, feeling the slow, fragile rhythm beneath his palm. He closed his eyes and remembered Cheri's voice the night she'd healed him: *Mercy doesn't command the world, Joe. It invites it to breathe again.*

Heat spread from his chest outward. The air filled with the faint scent of rain on stone. The fire in the hearth flared brighter but not hotter. The boy gasped, coughed, then drew a long, steady breath.

The mother covered her mouth. "He—he's—"

Joe: "Sleeping. Let him."

Outside, people gathered at the doorway. They expected spectacle; instead, they saw a man wiping soot from his hands, as ordinary as any laborer.

Villager: "What magic was that?"
Joe: "The kind that listens first."

♥ ✳ ♥ ✳ ♥

Confrontation

By nightfall, half the village waited in the square. The priest stood before them, voice trembling with both authority and uncertainty.

Priest: "You bring strange fire, stranger. The old flames protected us once."
Joe: "Did they? Or did they just keep you afraid?"
Priest: "Fear kept us alive!"
Joe: "No. Fear kept you from living."

He stepped closer, and the glow from the nearby torches softened instead of flared.

Joe: "Fire doesn't choose between good or evil. It just reveals what's there. You decide what burns."

He touched the nearest torch. The flame folded inward, turning pale gold. The people gasped as warmth—not heat—spilled over them like sunlight through cloud. The fear that clung to the air began to loosen.

A woman in the crowd whispered, *"Kindness like fire."*
The words spread from mouth to mouth until the square filled with murmurs that sounded almost like prayer.

Restoration

Over the next days, Brimvale changed in small, stubborn ways.
They stopped leaving food at the old shrines. They started feeding the living instead.
Children played in the square again; laughter cracked the hard shell of silence.
When Joe left, they gave him bread wrapped in cloth and a small carved symbol — a circle crossed by a single rising line.

Priest (quietly): "It means light remembered."

Joe: "Then keep remembering."

He tucked it into his pack beside the journal Cheri had once urged him to keep.
The fire within him pulsed once, steady and strong.
He whispered into the wind,

"We're both doing it, Cheri. One village at a time."

Far to the south, in a field just waking to spring, the pendant at her throat warmed in answer.

Spring crept northward slowly that year, as if unsure the world still deserved it.
The snow that once buried the valleys melted in hesitant rivulets, carving silver veins through the ash.
Joe followed those veins south, boots sinking into thawing soil, the air thick with the smell of wet pine and smoke.

Everywhere he walked, something shifted.
Rivers once blackened with soot ran clearer. Birds

returned to trees that had stood empty since the temple fires. Fields left fallow began to green again without seed. The people called it *the Dawnfire's trail*; Joe called it mercy remembering its road.

At night, he wrote by the light of a small camp-fire, the journal resting on his knee.
His handwriting had changed — broader, freer, as though the words no longer feared their own meaning.

He wrote of the faces he'd met, the laughter that came back too quietly to notice at first, the way warmth could heal where medicine could not.

And between every page, he left a space —
for her.

Echoes in the Water

He reached the River Serin again at dusk, its surface rippling gold.
Kneeling to fill his flask, he froze. The reflection

staring back at him shimmered — not with his face, but with a flash of light that pulsed once, soft and steady, like a heartbeat carried on water.

His chest mark warmed beneath his hand. The feeling was unmistakable: not pain, not heat, but presence.

Joe (whispering): "Cheri…?"

The river answered in ripples. No words, just movement — but it was enough.
He smiled through sudden tears, muttering,

"So that's how you found me before. Through water. Through mercy."

He stayed there until the moon rose, sketching the shimmer into his journal's margin, labeling it only *Her Light — Still Moving.*

The World Awakens

Further south, near the marsh where Cheri tended Patty's garden, the pendant at her throat flared the same moment he touched the water.

The herbs around her bent toward the glow, leaves trembling as if they heard a distant voice calling their name.

Patty looked up from her weaving.

Patty: "What is it?"

Cheri (smiling): "The world just remembered him."

She didn't explain further. Some things were better left to faith than to reason.

Convergence

For days afterward, stories began to crisscross the roads like migrating birds.

Traders from the north spoke of a man whose fire healed frostbite.

Farmers from the south spoke of a woman whose song made grain rise twice in a season.

By the time these tales met halfway in a crossroads tavern, they were inseparable: *Faithheart and Dawnfire,* two halves of the same mercy, walking different roads that led to the same sunrise.

Joe heard one such story from a group of hunters near the valley rim.

They spoke of a southern healer who wore a pendant that glowed when she prayed.

He didn't interrupt; he only listened until they slept, then sat awake beside the embers, tracing the shape of her name into the dirt.

Joe: "Keep calling me, Cheri. I'll follow the warmth."

The Song in the Wind

The closer he came to the midlands, the more
the world seemed to sing.
Wind through the grass hummed low, like the memory
of her voice.
Sometimes he caught the faint echo of laughter — not
real sound, but the impression of it, the way scent
lingers after rain.

He stopped once on a ridge overlooking miles
of green, closed his eyes, and felt the rhythm between
his heart and the pulse beneath the soil.
Two beats, in harmony.
Two paths, converging unseen.

When he opened his eyes, the horizon was no
longer gray but edged with gold.
The dawn was coming from the south — her direction.
He shouldered his pack, tightened his cloak, and
started walking toward it.

Chapter Thirteen – Where Mercy Meets

"Two lights, long apart, do not collide.
They recognize each other, and the dark between them
forgets its purpose."

The Summons

The wind came first—a hot, unnatural gust that bent trees backward and carried the taste of copper and ash.

Joe looked up from the road and saw a wall of smoke swelling over the southern hills. The horizon flickered orange, pulsing like a heartbeat against the gray sky. For an instant he was a child again, standing before the temple gates while the world burned. His breath caught, but the fear didn't take him this time. He pressed his palm to the healed scar over his heart. The warmth there wasn't pain—it was a summons.

Cheri.

The pulse in his chest answered some faraway rhythm. He started running.

♥ ✳ ♥ ✳ ♥

The Opposite Side of the Flame

Cheri saw the same smoke from the valley below. The pendant against her throat flared white-hot, and the air around her hummed like a string drawn too tight. When the first tongues of flame leapt the ridge, villagers screamed and scattered toward the stream with buckets.

Patty reached for her sleeve, shouting something lost in the wind. Cheri shook her head. "No—there's something deeper. It's not just fire."

She grabbed her cloak and sprinted uphill into the smoke.

The heat was blinding. Each breath seared her lungs. Still she lifted both hands, whispering the words

Tess had taught her in dreams. Light gathered around her fingers and broke outward in a shimmering arc; where it touched, the grass hissed and cooled, the fire stalling for a heartbeat before surging around the edges again. She poured everything she had into it—faith, fear, mercy—but the blaze devoured her effort as if it were nothing more than dew.

Across the valley, unseen, another light began to answer.

Joe in the Inferno

He fought his way through the choking haze, using gusts of power to push smoke aside just long enough to breathe. Each time he tried to quench a burning tree, another ignited behind him. The flames were alive, mocking him—too fast, too hungry. He remembered the elders' whispers: *fire follows him, always.* For a heartbeat doubt slipped through.

Then the air shifted.

Through the roar he heard something like a song carried on the wind—a woman's voice, distant but steady, weaving prayer into the storm. The mark on his chest responded instantly, its rhythm syncing to that unseen melody.

"Cheri," he gasped, realization cutting through smoke.

He turned toward the sound and hurled his will forward. The fire between them split open in a corridor of light.

♥ ✳ ♥ ✳ ♥

The Meeting of Mercy and Flame

They saw each other at the same moment— two figures framed in opposite halves of the burning valley, both glowing, both refusing to yield. The fire curved around them as if uncertain which one to obey.

Joe raised his hand across the distance; Cheri mirrored him. The moment their gestures aligned, the world seemed to inhale.

Light burst from her pendant, streaming toward him like water drawn uphill. His chestmark flared, answering with fire that wasn't destruction but purpose. When the two lights touched, they didn't cancel—they multiplied. The blaze convulsed outward in a spiral of gold and crimson, a storm folding in on itself.

Thunder rolled.

Wind howled backward through the valley, sucking oxygen from the fire's heart. The flames collapsed, not dying but kneeling, coalescing into a single column that blazed white before imploding in a shower of rain and embers.

Steam swept across the hills. The roar faded to a deep, resonant hum that trembled through the soil. Villagers on the far ridge dropped to their knees, covering their faces as heat became light, and light became silence.

When the air finally cleared, Joe and Cheri stood at the epicenter, hands clasped, surrounded by a circle of glassed earth cooling under the first gentle rainfall.

They didn't yet realize what they had done. The fire was gone, the village saved—but the miracle had only just begun.

For a long moment there was only the sound of rain.
It fell soft and clean, hissing against the still-warm earth, washing soot from the hills until rivulets of gray ran down into the gullies. Steam drifted like ghosts through the valley, curling around the two figures who stood at its center.

Joe and Cheri didn't move. Their hands were still joined, their breaths still caught between disbelief and relief. The world had gone eerily still — the kind of stillness that follows prayer answered too quickly to comprehend.

Water dripped from Joe's hair onto the blackened soil. He looked down, chest heaving, and saw that the fire had stopped within a perfect circle around them — as if the world itself had chosen where to draw its line. Outside that circle lay ruin: ash, char, and smoke. Inside, the ground steamed but lived, faint veins of green already threading through the soot.

He turned to Cheri. She was trembling — not from fear, but from release. Her hair clung in damp curls to her cheeks; the light of her pendant had dimmed to a gentle pulse. When she met his eyes, the exhaustion gave way to something older and stronger than either of them could name.

Joe (softly): "You came through the fire."
Cheri: "So did you."
Joe: "I thought I'd lost you once."
Cheri: "You never did."

The words should have been impossible in the hush that followed, but somehow they felt true. Every ember that cooled around them seemed to echo the same thought: not lost — found.

The Recognition

He reached up, brushing a streak of soot from her face, and her lips parted on a breath that was half-laughter, half-sob.

Cheri: "You're still glowing."

He looked down — his chestmark shimmered faintly beneath the torn edge of his shirt. "So are you."

When his hand found hers again, the warmth spread between them, not as flame but as heartbeat. The air thickened, alive with that pulse. Their shadows blurred until they no longer knew where one ended and the other began.

For a heartbeat they only stood there, two halves of a single mercy rediscovered.

The Kiss

Wind moved again, gentle this time, sweeping smoke away to reveal the gray-gold sky. Light from her pendant and his mark joined, wrapping them in the soft glow of dawn.
For a long moment neither spoke. They simply breathed the same air, the same trembling relief.

Then Joe whispered, his voice low, reverent:

Joe: "You were the mercy I couldn't find."
Cheri: "And you were the dawn that wouldn't die."

He lifted his hand to her face, thumb tracing the tear that had carved a clean path through the soot. She leaned into his touch; the world tilted quietly toward them.

When their lips met, it wasn't desperate or hurried. It was the slow, certain meeting of two prayers spoken at the same time.

Light flared between them—not fire, not magic, but life remembering itself. It rolled outward in ripples that shimmered through the rain, sinking into soil and seed alike. The scent of ash faded beneath the smell of wet earth and growing things.

Grass pushed through blackened ground. Tiny green shoots uncurled in widening circles. The burned valley began to breathe again.

The Witnesses

At the ridge, the villagers who had come with buckets and wet cloths froze where they stood. They had expected ruin. Instead they saw light and water mingling, the flames gone, the land shimmering gold beneath a silver rain.

A child pointed.

Child: "They're glowing!"

An elder beside her bowed, voice shaking.

Elder: "The song that stays…"

The words caught and carried, whispered from mouth to mouth, soft as prayer: *the song that stays, the heart of the dawn, the mercy that returns.*

No one dared to step forward. They simply watched as the two figures stood in the rain, unaware of their own radiance, unaware that where their feet touched, a garden was already blooming. Wildflowers broke through soot in colors no one had seen before. Vines traced spirals in the wet soil, forming the faint outline of a heart encircled by flame — a pattern that would never fade no matter how many seasons passed.

After the Light

Joe drew back only far enough to rest his forehead against hers. Rain slid between them, cool and clean. The glow between chestmark and pendant dimmed to a steady ember, still pulsing in harmony.

Joe: "We found each other."
Cheri: "We never stopped."

Their laughter mingled with the sound of rain, small and human after the grandeur of what had just passed. The fire was gone. The fear was gone. Only the heartbeat remained — theirs, and the world's, at last in rhythm again.

High above, thunder rolled, soft as applause.

Neither of them noticed that the ash at their feet was turning to fertile soil, that buds were already opening where the light had touched. They wouldn't see the valley bloom the next morning, when the villagers returned to find flowers where flame had been. But the story would spread — of the fire that knelt, the rain that sang, and the two who brought life back to the land.

The story would be called *The Song That Stays.*

The Road Home

The rain eased into a gentle mist that blurred the edges of everything it touched.
Steam curled from the valley, winding through the air like memory. Joe and Cheri walked hand in hand down the muddy road, the smell of smoke still clinging to their clothes, the rhythm of their joined steps slow and steady. Neither spoke; words would have felt too small for what they had just survived.

Behind them, the circle where the fire had bowed low still glowed faintly. They didn't look back, but the villagers did. Those who had fled now stood on the ridge, watching green push through black soil—the first fragile shoots rising where flame had devoured.

The pattern they formed — heart within flame — shimmered like a promise the world was keeping for itself.

> *They healed the fire.*
> *The land blooms beneath them.*
> *The Song That Stays.*

The whispers carried on the wind, reaching the village before they did.

At the Gate

By the time Joe and Cheri reached the village road, people were gathering, drawn by the sound of bells and distant singing. Patty was the first to appear, skirts soaked, hair plastered to her face, eyes wide as she ran toward them. She stopped short a few steps away, staring at the soot-streaked man beside Cheri.

Patty: "Cheri, don't tell me you walked into that fire again — and who on earth is *this?*"

Her gaze flicked between them, taking in their clasped hands, the faint shimmer of light still pulsing between their fingers.

Cheri smiled, exhausted but radiant.

Cheri: "Patty, this is Joe. The one I told you about — the man the Temple feared and the river defended."

Patty blinked, breath catching. "The *Heart of the Dawn?*"

Her voice cracked on the title, halfway between disbelief and awe. Then, with a quick shake of her head, she muttered,

Patty: "Well … he looks less terrifying up close."

Before either could reply, she stepped forward and pulled them both into a damp, fierce embrace.

Patty: "If you're the reason my girl's alive, then you're family. But next time mercy calls, maybe answer with words instead of wildfire."

Joe laughed softly, breathless. "I'll do my best."

Patty drew back, tears cutting clean lines down her soot-streaked cheeks. She studied the two of them for a long moment, then said quietly,

Patty: "All my life I've said faith was for dreamers and children. But if I just watched the world burn itself out and come back green …"

Her voice trembled; she finished with a shaky laugh.

Patty: "… then maybe it's time I start believing too."

Cheri reached for her hand, squeezing it. "Maybe faith was believing *with* your eyes open all along."

Patty smiled through the tears. "Then I'll keep them wide open."

The Square

The rest of the village poured in behind her — farmers, children, elders — their fear melting into laughter and praise. Some carried buckets, some torches, others simply came to see. When they caught sight of Cheri and Joe standing together, a wave of quiet spread through the crowd. A few began to kneel, but Joe quickly raised his hands.

Joe: "Please — don't. We're just …"

Cheri touched his arm and turned toward the people. Her voice carried clearly over the soft patter of rain.

Cheri: "This is Joe — the Heart of the Dawn, yes — but he's also just a man who remembered that mercy burns brighter than fear. What happened out there wasn't power. It was love doing what it was meant to."

The murmurs fell still. Dozens of eyes turned toward Joe, waiting. He hesitated, then said simply,

Joe: "We didn't stop the fire. Mercy did. We only listened."

A hush followed, then someone started clapping. Another joined. Then the square erupted in sound — applause, laughter, tears, voices lifted together. A farmer raised his hands and began an old harvest tune; others picked it up, changing the words as they sang:

> *Mercy stays, mercy stays,*
> *Heart of dawn, Lightheart's blaze …*

The refrain caught and spread until even the rain seemed to fall in rhythm with it.

Cheri looked up at Joe, eyes bright. "They've already made it a song."

He smiled, shaking his head. "Then maybe it's true."

The Walk Home

When the celebration began to swell, Joe leaned toward her ear.

Joe: "Before they decide we're saints, maybe we should find somewhere quieter."
Cheri (smiling): "Good idea."

They slipped from the square, still hand in hand, following the narrow path along the river. The clouds were breaking, the setting sun bleeding gold through the mist. The water shimmered beside them, a mirror for the light they carried.

Joe: "Do you think they'll remember it the way it happened?"

Cheri: "Maybe not. But they'll remember that it *happened*. That's enough."

Behind them, the bells rang again, joined by singing and laughter. By the time they reached the bend in the road, the sound had softened to a hum. The rain had stopped completely. Where their footprints met the mud, tiny flowers had begun to bloom.

Neither of them noticed. They only knew the warmth of each other's hands and the strange, beautiful truth of walking home through a world that had finally learned how to breathe again.

As the path curved toward the edge of the village, Cheri slowed, tugging Joe gently toward a low stone wall half-hidden by wild vines. Two figures waited there, faces lit by the amber glow of a single lantern — Janis and Michael. They rose as the pair approached.

Janis: "We were afraid the stories had already taken you."

Cheri (smiling): "They almost did."

Michael glanced between them, eyes widening at the faint shimmer still lingering on their hands. "So it's true then. You stopped the fire."

Joe (quietly): "The fire stopped itself. We just listened."

For a moment, none of them spoke. The lantern flame flickered, painting their faces in gold and shadow. Then Janis stepped closer, resting a hand on Cheri's arm. "Whatever it was, the village will remember tonight as the first time hope felt real again."

Cheri looked at Joe, her expression soft. "Then maybe that's where healing begins."

Michael grinned, the edge of disbelief melting into admiration. "If that's healing, I can't wait to see what you do next."

They all laughed — quiet, tired, and genuine. The kind of laughter that came only after surviving something that should have ended them.

When the moment faded, Cheri leaned against Joe's shoulder. "Come on," she said softly. "Patty will scold us if we don't eat before the whole village steals the supper."
Joe smiled, nodding. "Lead the way, Lightheart."

Together, they turned toward the lantern-lit road, the others falling in step behind them as the night settled gentle and whole around their small band — the beginning of a family the world would someday call *the Circle of Dawn.*

Chapter Fourteen – Building a Home

"The world is healed not only by miracles,but by hands that choose to stay."

Morning in a Reborn World

Morning came soft and slow, the kind that felt earned. Light drifted through the shutters of Patty's small guest room, carrying the scent of bread and dew-wet earth. Joe blinked awake, half expecting to find the fire still burning, the world still trembling. Instead there was only stillness, and the gentle creak of the village settling into life again.

He sat up, the unfamiliar weight of a roof over his head pressing lightly on his chest. A home. Not a cave, not a ruined hall, not the open road — just four walls and a quilt that smelled faintly of lavender. It felt wrong and right at the same time.

Outside, laughter floated through the window. Somewhere a child shouted about "the glowing garden," and another voice hushed them as if even joy might break the spell. Joe smiled, rubbing the sleep from his eyes. He hadn't realized how tired he'd been until rest had finally found him.

Patty's knock came sharp and unapologetic.

Patty: "You planning to sleep through a reborn world?"

Joe (groaning): "Was hoping to."

The door opened before he could protest further. Patty stood there with her hands on her hips and flour streaked on her cheek.

Patty: "You can't fix every broken fence before breakfast, Heart of Dawn."

Joe: "I wasn't planning to."

Patty: "Good. Because I already assigned you to the well team. And don't argue — the rope snapped last week, and you've got arms enough to help."

She left as abruptly as she came, muttering something about "heroes with bed hair." Joe chuckled, ran a hand through the offending curls, and reached for his boots.

The square outside shimmered with life. Villagers carried buckets, hammered boards, and strung new lantern lines from post to post. Every task was ordinary, yet none of it felt small. The land itself seemed to hum beneath their feet — soil rich, air sweet with the scent of renewal.

Joe joined the repair crew at the well. The first few stares still lingered on him a moment too long, but they weren't fearful anymore. Respect, maybe. Curiosity. Gratitude. He could live with that.

A boy no older than twelve handed him a coil of rope, eyes wide.

Boy: "Is it true you made the fire kneel?"

Joe (smiling): "It knelt for mercy, not for me."

The boy frowned, then nodded as if storing the answer for later. By midday, Joe had patched two fences, repaired a gate, and helped an old man straighten a leaning porch post. Each act felt like prayer disguised as work.

When he paused to wipe sweat from his brow, he saw Cheri across the road kneeling beside a broken planter, coaxing new shoots from the blackened soil. Sunlight slid across her shoulders, catching in her hair. She looked up at him, smiling — that quiet, steady smile that seemed to see right through him and forgive everything she found there.

Joe's chest ached with something too vast to name.

Patty passed behind him carrying nails and muttered under her breath,

Patty: "If you're going to stare, at least make yourself useful and bring her water."

He did.

Cheri took the offered bucket, their fingers brushing. "You don't have to help with everything," she said softly.

Joe: "I know. I just don't know how not to."

Her laughter was light as wind chimes. "Then maybe start by building something for yourself."

That thought lingered long after she returned to her work. By sunset, Joe found himself standing near the edge of the village, staring at a small cottage half-collapsed from the fire's smoke and heat. The owner had left years ago, Patty explained — it was free to anyone willing to rebuild.

Joe traced the doorway, rough wood beneath his fingertips, and whispered to no one,

"Maybe I could stay."

The words felt strange, dangerous, holy.

Behind him, the bells began to ring for evening prayers. For the first time in years, he didn't keep walking.

The next morning dawned warm and bright, the air heavy with sawdust and the smell of rain-soaked earth. Joe had barely finished sweeping out the cottage when Cheri appeared at the doorway carrying two mugs of tea and a bundle of wildflowers.

Cheri: "For the windows."
Joe (grinning): "You're assuming there'll be windows."
Cheri: "Then I'll plant them outside. The flowers don't mind where they bloom."

♥ ✳ ♥ ✳ ♥

Hands That Heal Together

She stepped past him, sunlight chasing her into the dim interior. The place was rough — smoke-stained beams, half a roof missing, the floor uneven where roots had grown through the boards. But in that light, it didn't feel ruined anymore.

Joe leaned against the doorframe, watching her trace her fingers along the cracked wall as though greeting an old friend.

Cheri: "You'll make it beautiful."
Joe: "I'm better at tearing things down than building them."
Cheri: "Then we'll learn together."

They started with furniture — or tried to. Michael and Janis, the village carpenters, offered them tools and far too much advice. Joe picked up a saw like a soldier handling a relic; Cheri just laughed and handed him a hammer.

Michael: "Start simple. A chair never bites back."
Cheri: "You haven't met Joe's chairs yet."

By midday the yard looked like a battlefield of wood shavings and crooked legs. Joe knelt beside his project, frowning in concentration, while Cheri sat cross-legged on the grass, carving an intricate sunburst into her chair's backrest.

Joe (pretending offense): "You're decorating before it stands?"

Cheri: "Faith first, structure later."

Joe: "That's backwards."

Cheri: "Exactly."

Her smile disarmed him every time. She had a way of making even failure feel like progress.

When his chair finally held its balance, slightly uneven but proud, he caught her watching him — chin resting on her hand, eyes bright.

Joe: "What?"

Cheri: "You looked happy. I don't think I've seen that before."

He stared down at the chair, cheeks warming. "Maybe I forgot how."

Cheri (softly): "Then keep building. You'll remember."

That evening, the four of them shared supper outside the workshop. Michael told stories about the first bridge he ever built; Janis teased him for how quickly it collapsed. The laughter came easy, the kind that filled the air like music.

As twilight deepened, lanterns flickered to life across the square. Cheri and Joe sat side by side, their mismatched chairs angled toward the sunset. Between them rested a single loaf of bread and two cups of tea gone cold.

Joe: "Not bad for beginners."
Cheri: "The chairs?"
Joe: "Us."

She smiled into the fading light, brushing a curl of hair from her face.

Cheri: "Maybe what's built in mercy doesn't need to be perfect."
Joe: "Then we're halfway to saints."
Cheri: "Don't ruin it."

Laughter again — quiet, honest, shared.

When the lanterns finally dimmed and the night pressed close around them, neither moved to leave. The air smelled of cedar and hope, and for once, Joe didn't think about the next road or the next burden. He only thought about the woman beside him and the sound of her laughter in the dark.

Lanterns flickered across the village square long after the laughter had faded. The night was clear, the stars sharp and bright above the rooftops. Janis worked quietly at her table, stringing ribbons through paper lanterns for the coming festival. Cheri sat across from her, chin in her hands, the half-finished lantern in front of her long forgotten.

Janis watched her for a while, pretending not to notice the sighs that kept escaping. Finally, she set down her spool of thread.

Janis: "You've been staring at that lantern for half an hour. Planning to light it with your thoughts?"

Cheri blinked, caught. "Sorry, I was thinking."

Janis (teasing): "About wood grain and rope tension, no doubt. Or a certain carpenter's new apprentice with eyes like stormlight?"

Cheri laughed, hiding her face in her hands. "I don't know what you're talking about."

Janis leaned forward on her elbows, voice gentler. "You used to look at the world like it might vanish if you blinked. Now you look at him like the world just remembered how to stay."

Cheri hesitated. "I don't even know what this is. Maybe it's just gratitude — or relief — or..."
Her voice trailed off. The lantern light wavered between them, painting gold in her hair.

Janis: "Gratitude doesn't make your hands shake when someone smiles at you."

Cheri gave a small, helpless laugh. "It shouldn't be this easy. Loving him feels like breathing, and that frightens me."

Janis: "Maybe it should. Maybe that's how you know it's real — when love doesn't ask to be earned."

For a long moment neither spoke. The crickets sang outside, soft as memory.

Cheri finally whispered, "He's still carrying so much. The things the Temple did to him — the lies they told. I see it every time he hesitates to reach for joy. I just want to show him that mercy isn't a word — it's a home."

Janis's throat tightened. "Then I think you already have."

Cheri blinked, surprised. "Have what?"

Janis: "Built it. The home he needed."

The House That Waited for Them

Silence settled, warm and heavy. Janis reached across the table and touched Cheri's hand, her thumb brushing over the faint ink stain still smudged from the journal they'd been copying together earlier.

Janis (softly): "If you ever doubt it, watch how he looks at you. That's not a man finding mercy. That's a man who already has."

Cheri smiled through the tears she hadn't realized were there.

Cheri: "Then maybe faith was always meant to look like this."

Janis squeezed her hand once more. "Maybe it was."

Outside, a single lantern drifted loose from its string, carried upward on a slow, golden wind. Both women watched it rise until it vanished into the night — a quiet promise floating toward morning.

The sun was barely above the hills when Joe made his way to Michael's workshop. The air was cool and sweet, thick with the scent of pine and beeswax. He could hear Janis humming inside — a slow, wordless tune that fit the rhythm of sanding wood smooth.

He hesitated at the doorway, one hand on the frame. She looked up immediately, as if she'd been expecting him.

Janis: "You're early."
Joe (half-smiling): "Couldn't sleep. Figured I'd earn breakfast."

She nodded toward a pile of rough boards.

Janis: "You can start with those. They've been waiting for a man with too much energy."

He laughed softly and went to work beside her, the sound of the plane and rasp filling the silence between them. For a while, they said nothing — only worked, the way people do when words might spill more truth than they intend.

After a few minutes, Janis glanced over.

Janis: "You've been looking at her like a man about to jump from a cliff."

Joe froze, hand tightening on the plane. "That obvious?"

Janis: "To anyone with eyes."

He set the tool down and leaned against the bench, staring at the curls of wood scattered like ribbons across the floor.

Joe: "I was thinking of asking her to marry me."

Janis said nothing, just waited. He took a breath, the words coming slow.

Joe: "But then I start thinking about what I've done… what I was. The Temple called me the Destroyer for a reason. I don't know if I have the right to ask someone like her to tie her life to mine."

Janis brushed the dust from her palms, voice gentle but firm.

Janis: "You know what I see when you talk about her?"

Joe (quietly): "What?"

Janis: "A man who's already tied his life to hers —
he just hasn't found the courage to tell her yet."

He smiled faintly. "I wanted to do it right.
Something special. She deserves that."

Janis: "Special isn't about candles or speeches. It's
about truth."
Joe: "And what if the truth scares her?"
Janis: "Then it's still truth. And she's stronger than
fear."

He looked up at her, meeting her steady eyes.

Joe: "You sound like you know her pretty well."
Janis: "Well enough to know she'd say yes if you ever
stopped second-guessing mercy."

He huffed a laugh, running a hand through his hair.
"You make it sound simple."

Janis (smiling): "It is. That's what makes it
terrifying."

They worked a while longer, the conversation
trailing off into quiet companionship. The morning

light slanted through the window, catching the dust in slow, golden motion.

As he gathered his tools, Janis said softly,

Janis: "Joe?"

Joe: "Yeah?"

Janis: "When you ask her… don't try to be anyone else. She already said yes in her heart a long time ago. The rest is just waiting to catch up."

He paused, throat tight. "Thank you."

Janis: "Go find your courage before the market opens. I've seen what happens when you two get near flour."

Walls Built With Mercy

He blinked. "Flour?"

Janis (grinning): "You'll see."

Joe had never planned anything romantic in his life.
Not properly.
Battle strategies, sure. Rationing for travel, yes. But a proposal?
That was a different kind of courage.

By dawn he was already pacing the cottage, a folded scrap of parchment in his hand — the plan. He'd written it down the night before in nervous, uneven lines:

Proposal Plan

Borrow blanket from Patty (wash first).

Ask Michael for bread and honey.

Wildflowers — not the ones near the outhouse.

Riverbank — same place Cheri found the herons.

Wait for sunset. Try not to panic.

Ask properly. Breathe.

He read it three times, then immediately lost his nerve halfway through item two.

Patty found him rearranging the same three apples on the table like a man negotiating peace with produce.

Patty: "You're making that poor fruit nervous."
Joe (startled): "I'm— it's for a picnic."
Patty: "A picnic? With Cheri?"
Joe (nodding, sheepish): "If she says yes."
Patty: "To the picnic or to you?"
Joe: "Hopefully both."

Patty stared at him for a beat, then sighed, hands on hips.

Patty: "You'll need better bait than apples. I'll send bread. And wine. For mercy's sake, at least one of you should be calm."

By midmorning, Joe had transformed the old riverbank into a kind of clumsy paradise — blanket smoothed, flowers scattered, a loaf of bread sliced unevenly beside a small wooden box he'd carved himself.
Inside was a simple ring, silver brushed with gold —

not perfect, but his hands had shaped it. That was enough.

He rehearsed what he'd say:

"Cheri, I don't know how to deserve you, but I'd like to spend my life trying."

Then again:

"Cheri, when you laugh, the world remembers how to heal."

He groaned aloud. "No, that sounds ridiculous."

Birds scattered from the reeds at his voice. He rubbed his face, muttering, "Maybe just Hi."

For a while he sat there in the quiet, heart thudding like the echo of distant drums.
Everything about this place felt sacred — not because of magic, but because of her.

When he finally stood, brushing the dirt from his knees, he smiled to himself. "All right. Just find her before I lose the courage."

The walk into the village was shorter than he remembered. Market day had filled the square with color and sound — ribbons fluttering, barrels rolling, merchants shouting cheerful insults at one another. He spotted her immediately: Cheri, near the baker's stall, hair loose in the wind, arms full of herbs and laughter.

He froze. His heart said, Now.

His brain said, Run.

The square was alive with motion — laughter, bartering, the metallic ring of coin and clatter of crates. Joe edged through the crowd, trying to look casual while carrying the carved ring box like it might explode.
Every step closer to Cheri made his pulse louder.

He rehearsed one last time under his breath:

"Cheri, I know I'm not the man you expected, but I'd spend every dawn trying to deserve you."
He winced. Too formal. Too Temple.

By the time he reached the baker's stall, his throat
had dried to sand.

Cheri turned just then, smiling bright as the morning.

Cheri: "Joe! You came into town after all. Patty
said you were hiding by the river."

Joe (fumbling): "Not hiding. Preparing. For…
something."

The baker — a cheerful man with arms like tree
trunks — was hauling a new sack of flour from the
wagon.

Joe, desperate to look helpful, stepped forward to take
it from him.

The Circle Gathers

Joe: "Here, let me—"

The seam split.

A white explosion filled the square. The world
vanished in a blizzard of flour.

Children screamed with delight; adults coughed and waved their hands.

When the dust cleared, Joe stood ghost-pale from head to boots, eyes blinking through powder.

Cheri was bent over laughing — the kind that stole her breath and doubled her over.

He could only stare, mortified and helplessly in love.

Joe: "That— wasn't supposed to happen."

Cheri (gasping): "Clearly."

Joe (panicked): "I had a whole plan. The river. The blanket. Bread. A speech."

Cheri: "A speech?"

Joe: "Yes, a—" He stopped, realizing the entire market was now watching.

He swallowed hard, reached into his pocket, and pulled out the flour-coated ring box. It slipped once in his trembling fingers before he caught it.

Joe (blurting): "I was going to ask you to marry me!"

The crowd went silent. Even the baker froze, white dust still drifting between them like snow.

Cheri blinked, eyes wide, cheeks streaked with flour and surprise.

Cheri: "Here? Now?"
Joe: "No! I mean— yes. I mean it's not how I meant it to go, but—"

He sighed, voice breaking into laughter and surrender.

Joe: "Cheri, I'm a disaster. But if you'll let me, I'll spend the rest of my life being your disaster."

A heartbeat of stillness.
Then Cheri stepped forward, closing the space between them, and placed a flour-dusted finger against his lips.

Cheri: "You just did."

The square erupted — laughter, cheers, applause.
Someone shouted, "About time!"
Joe stood frozen until she leaned up and kissed his

cheek, leaving a perfect white print where her lips touched.

Cheri (smiling): "Guess we're both marked now."

The baker raised his hands, booming, "Drinks on me — for the happy couple!"
The crowd cheered louder, and Joe could only laugh, dizzy with relief and love and the sweet smell of bread rising all around them.

Evening

By the time they escaped the celebration, dusk had painted the river gold.
Cheri carried the crooked ring box, turning it over in her hands.

Cheri: "You planned all this?"
Joe: "Not… exactly like this."
Cheri: "It's perfect."

He looked at her in disbelief. "Perfect?"

Cheri: "Because it's you. And because mercy never waits for plans."

She slipped the ring onto her finger — too loose, a
little bent, shining like starlight anyway.
Then she stood on tiptoe and kissed him softly.

Cheri: "Now promise me you'll still take me to the
river tomorrow. I want to see the place you meant to
ask me."
Joe: "I will."

They walked home through the fading light, hand
in hand, leaving white footprints where the flour clung
to their boots.
Behind them, the bells of the village chimed one by
one, carrying their laughter all the way to the fields that
had once burned.

Patty found him just after nightfall.
The cottage glowed faintly from the single lantern on
the table, and Joe was still sweeping up flour from the
floorboards, muttering about how it "followed him
home."
He turned when the door creaked open.

Joe: "If it's about the mess, I swear I tried—"
Patty: "You asked her."

Her tone wasn't angry, but it wasn't soft either.
She stepped inside, arms folded, eyes sharp enough to
cut through the dim.

Patty: "Half the village saw it. The baker hasn't
stopped talking. And now my Cheri—"
She stopped, jaw tightening.
Patty: "My Cheri is promising herself to the man they
used to call the Destroyer."

Joe set the broom aside, shoulders heavy.

Joe: "I know what they called me. And I know
what I was."
Patty: "Then why would you let her—"
Joe: "Because she chose me anyway."

The words hung in the air, plain and unguarded.
Patty's lips pressed thin. She turned toward the table,
tracing a finger through the thin layer of white dust still
clinging there.

Patty: "Do you love her?"

Joe: "More than I understand how to say."

Patty: "And what happens when that fire of yours flares again? When the world whispers that you're danger wrapped in mercy?"

Joe: "Then I'll remind it what mercy looks like."
He took a step closer, voice steady.
Joe: "I can't promise perfection. But I can promise her truth. Every day. No more lies. No more running."

Where Dawn Learns to Stay

Patty studied him for a long time. The lines around her eyes softened, and when she finally spoke again, her voice had dropped to almost a whisper.

Patty: "You sound like her."

He smiled faintly. "She sounds like faith."

Something in her broke then — not in pain, but in surrender.
She reached up, brushing flour from his shoulder, shaking her head.

Patty: "You're a terrible sight for a man about to be married. Look at you — still covered in dough like a ghost come to supper."

He laughed, relieved, and the sound loosened the air between them.
Patty sighed, pulling out a chair and sitting down heavily.

Patty: "You know, when I first met her, she was all fire and stubbornness. She'd fight the wind if it blew wrong. But you…"
She looked up at him.
Patty: "You make her calm without dimming her light. I didn't think that was possible."

Joe (quietly): "She makes me believe I can be good."

Patty nodded, tears shining in her tired eyes.

Patty: "Then maybe I was wrong about fire. Maybe it can warm instead of burn."

She rose, crossing to him, and laid a calloused hand against his cheek — a mother's touch, testing and blessing at once.

Patty: "Don't you hurt her, Joe. Not in word, not in deed, not even by silence. Promise me that."

Joe: "I promise."

She smiled, the first real smile since she'd entered.

Patty: "Good. Because if you do, I'll raise the whole village against you."

He chuckled, and she turned toward the door. Before stepping out, she paused and looked back.

Patty: "For what it's worth, she's always been a fool for miracles. I suppose it makes sense she'd fall for one."

The door closed softly behind her.

Joe stood for a long while, listening to the night
settle — the crickets, the whisper of the river, the echo
of her words.

When he finally looked down, a faint trail of flour
footprints led from the door to where he stood. He
smiled.

Joe (to himself): "Maybe miracles aren't so bad
after all."

The cottage was still when Joe returned.

The lantern on the table had burned low, its flame a
small golden heartbeat inside the glass.

Cheri was asleep in one of their unfinished chairs, her
head tipped back, a stray lock of hair caught in the
light.

Beside her sat the other chair — his — waiting, uneven
but sturdy, the pair facing each other like a promise not
yet spoken.

Joe stopped in the doorway, smiling softly.

The air smelled of wood and fresh bread, of warmth
that didn't need tending.

For the first time in years, the silence didn't accuse

him.
It welcomed him.

He crossed the floor quietly, set the broom aside,
and crouched beside her.
Her hand hung over the armrest, fingers open, palm
upward — as if she'd fallen asleep reaching for
something she never stopped believing in.
He took it gently, pressing his thumb over the faint
pulse there.

Joe (whispering): "Guess we'll finish these
tomorrow, Lightheart."

She murmured something in her sleep — his name,
maybe — and the lantern flame flickered in answer.
He brushed a thumb along her cheek, leaving the
faintest trace of flour from his sleeve.
It felt like the world's smallest vow.

Outside, dawn began to edge over the hills.
The sky blushed with the first pale gold of morning,
and the bells of the village started one by one — slow,
joyful, ringing across the valley.

The sound drifted through the half-open window, carrying laughter and footsteps and the hum of preparation.

The Festival of Light had begun.

Joe glanced toward the chairs again — hers with carved sunbursts along the back, his plain but solid beside it.
Together, they caught the dawn.
For a moment he imagined them both years from now, side by side by some quiet fire, still reaching for each other across the distance between.

He leaned down, pressed a kiss to her hair, and whispered:

Joe: "We're home."

Outside, the bells kept ringing — clear and bright — as if the whole world agreed.

Chapter Fifteen – Festival of Light

'When ash remembers how to bloom,

the bells teach morning how to sing.

Bind your mercy to the dawn—

before the hour grows wings.''

Morning Bells and Blossoms

Dawn arrived like a held-breath finally released.

For the first time since the fire, the valley was not gray.

Mist rolled low across fields that had once been black and hollowed, but now shimmered with soft gold blossoms that caught the newborn light. Dew glittered on every stem, diamonds ;eft by the night's quiet hands.

The bells began before the sun cleared the ridge—first one, then another, until the whole village seemed to ring awake. Doors opened, laughter tumbled into the chill air, and ribbons of color streamed from windows. A week ago they'd whispered; today they sang.

Joe stepped outside, rubbing the back of his neck. The air smelled of bread and lilacs and something electric he couldn't name. Children ran past carrying baskets of petals, one calling over her shoulder, "Heart of Dawn! Come hang the lanterns!"

He blinked at the nickname, half-smiling. "That one's going to stick, isn't it?"

From the lane below, Patty shouted back without looking up from her ladder.

"Might as well accept it! You name a miracle, it stays named!"

He laughed and took the offered spool of ribbon. Together they fastened bright streamers to the old archway that marked the square's entrance. The structure had been blackened by smoke months before; now vines climbed it again, heavy with bloom.

Cheri arrived with an armful of garlands, sunlight catching in her hair.

"You're tying those uneven again."

"I'm enhancing the rustic charm," Joe said, deadpan.

She bit back a smile. "The rustic charm is hanging upside-down."

They worked shoulder to shoulder, the kind of quiet companionship that needed no planning. When she hummed, petals along the garland unfurled wider, the blossoms following her voice. Joe pretended not to notice, but the sight of it—life answering her—made something ache in his chest.

Across the square, Janis and Michael tuned their instruments; vendors arranged honey-glazed fruit, spiced bread, and jars of wildflowers. The whole village moved as one rhythm. Hope had a sound again.

Patty straightened from her ladder, surveying their work.

"If this keeps up, you two will have to marry before sunset just to keep the world's balance straight."

Cheri flushed. "Patty!"

"I'm serious! The way the weather obeys you, might as well make it official."

Joe tried not to grin. "Let's not provoke the elements before breakfast."

They laughed, the moment stretching easy and bright. For the first time since he'd woken in that burned field, Joe realized he wasn't bracing for loss. The world felt fragile, yes—but alive, responsive, waiting.

He paused, looking east. The horizon gleamed with a thin line of silver, the same hue that had once surrounded Tess. It flickered and was gone, leaving only the sky, impossibly clear.

Mercy in Motion

Cheri followed his gaze. "What is it?"

"Nothing," he said after a beat. "Just thought I saw light move the wrong way."

"Maybe it was mercy checking her reflection," she teased, nudging his shoulder.

He smiled but didn't answer. Deep inside, the hum of their shared bond stirred—gentle, insistent. Something unseen was drawing closer.

Behind them, Patty clapped her hands.

"All right, Heart of Dawn, Lightheart, stop mooning and start hauling. We've a festival to raise before the day runs off without us!"

Joe tipped an invisible hat. "Yes, ma'am."

The bells rang again, brighter now, echoing off the hills. Lanterns caught the light, swinging like captured stars above the square. The valley, once ruined by fire, glowed like a promise kept—and beneath the laughter and song, a faint vibration whispered through the ground, as though the earth itself were tuning to some greater melody about to begin.

By mid-morning the square was a heartbeat. Every stall overflowed — honey cakes steaming on trays, ribbons fluttering from poles, fiddles chasing one another through sunlight. Laughter ran like water between the booths. For once, no one spoke of rebuilding or loss; today they built only joy.

Joe stood at the edge of it, half amazed. The last time he'd seen this many people in one place, they'd been fleeing fire. Now they were dancing in its ashes.

Cheri found him staring, pressed a flower garland into his hands.

Cheri: "Don't just watch — wear the miracle you made."

Joe: "Pretty sure you made most of it."

Cheri: "Then consider this teamwork."

She looped the garland over his shoulders before he could protest. The petals brushed his neck, cool and fragrant. Her smile left him more breathless than the crowd's cheering.

Someone struck the first chord of a reel, and the square erupted. Children leapt between adults, skirts and sleeves a whirl of color. Cheri seized Joe's hand before he could retreat.

Cheri: "You owe me one dance, Heart of Dawn."
Joe: "I have terrible rhythm."
Cheri: "Then mercy will keep time for you."

She pulled him into the circle. His steps stumbled at first, boots catching on cobblestones, but the rhythm was contagious. Soon he was laughing, matching her turns. Wherever their feet met, tiny green shoots broke through cracks in the stone. The onlookers gasped, then cheered louder.

Patty clapped from her bench, pretending to scold.

Patty: "Now you're sprouting weeds in my clean street!"

Joe (panting): "They're festive weeds!"

Janis lifted her voice above the fiddles, singing the new refrain she'd written that morning — a melody taken from Cheri's hum and Joe's heartbeat.

"Love stays longer than fire,
Light outlives the flame,
Mercy remembers the morning,
And calls the dawn by name."

The Return of the Wanderers

By the second verse, the whole square joined in. Even Joe, who never sang, found himself mouthing the words.

When the song ended, Cheri leaned close, cheeks flushed.

Cheri: "See? You can dance."
Joe: "Only when the ground forgives me."
Cheri: "It already has."

The fiddles shifted to a slower rhythm, and couples paired off. Joe and Cheri stepped aside, letting others whirl. They stood together beneath the arch they'd decorated that morning. The ribbons swayed above them like tongues of captured dawn.

Across the square, a tall traveler watched — Leron, dust from the road still on his cloak, and beside him a quiet young man with thoughtful eyes. Joe didn't see them yet. He was still watching Cheri, and the way the sunlight turned her hair into something the world could pray through.

Overhead, unseen by any but the birds, a faint shimmer rippled through the air — as if the sky itself were drawing a breath.

The dance was breaking up when a voice carried from the bridge at the edge of the square.

Voice: "If that's the man they call Heart of Dawn, he owes me two textbooks and an apology!"

Joe turned, squinting into the sun. For a heartbeat the shape was only glare and dust—then he laughed, disbelieving.

Joe: "Leron?"

The older man spread his arms and strode through the crowd, dusty cloak flying. "You didn't think I'd let you start a religion without me, did you?"

They collided in a rough embrace that turned quickly into back-slapping laughter. Villagers cheered, not knowing why; joy simply recognized its own echo.

When they pulled apart, Leron gestured to the quiet figure behind him—a tall, lean youth with ink-stained fingers and the posture of someone more used to libraries than road dust.

Leron: "This is Dalen. Used to share your dorm at the Temple—before they started calling you a myth."

Joe blinked, the memory surfacing: a boy always asking why even when no one wanted to answer.

Joe: "You grew taller."
Dalen: "And you, apparently, grew legendary."

He lifted a satchel and withdrew a small, leather-bound book. The edges were worn soft, the title pressed faintly in Joe's own handwriting.

Dalen: "I copied this from fragments left behind. We've been teaching from it in every village we pass. They call it The Teachings of the Dawn."

Joe took it carefully, like it might burn. Pages fluttered open—his own sketches and half-formed prayers, once scrawled in frustration, now illuminated with careful script and marginal notes.

Joe (quietly): "I never meant for anyone to read these."
Leron: "Then you shouldn't have written truth in them."

Leron grinned, unrepentant. "The world's starving for it. You dropped breadcrumbs of mercy, and people started following the trail."

Cheri stepped forward, eyes wide.

Cheri: "So the song's already spreading."
Leron: "Faster than plague, thank the stars. We followed whispers of miracles—fires quenched, waters healed. Every story ended here."

The Guest of Light

He looked around at the garlands, the laughter, the impossible green bursting from stone.

Leron (softly): "You did it, Joe. You proved them wrong."

Joe shook his head. "We did. You taught me half of this, remember?"

Leron chuckled. "I taught you how to dodge lectures. The rest came from someone higher—and maybe," he added, glancing toward the river where a silver flash of light skimmed the surface, "someone nearer."

Dalen followed his gaze but saw nothing.

Dalen: "We heard a voice on the wind the night before we found this place. It said, 'Go north, where mercy dances with flame.' I thought Leron was hearing things again."
Leron: "And yet here we are."

Patty bustled up, wiping her hands on her apron. "You two must be starving. Come eat before you faint from holiness."

The laughter returned easily. They joined the feast tables, trading stories until the sun leaned west. Music wove through their talk; every so often, Joe's eyes strayed toward the shimmer of the river, a quiet pulse beneath the merriment.

Somewhere out there, unseen, the Guest of Light was already walking the festival paths, her smile both proud and sorrowful.

Evening settled like a blessing.
Lanterns bloomed across the square, each flame mirrored in the river's glassy surface. Fiddles softened to gentler tunes; couples drifted toward the bridge to watch the reflections. It felt as though the valley itself were breathing again.

No one noticed the silver-haired woman at first.

She moved easily among them, neither guest nor stranger—helping a child relight a candle, steadying a tray when a vendor stumbled, repairing a musician's broken string with a touch that sparked faint gold. She asked no name, gave none. The villagers began calling her the Guest of Light, as if that had always been her title.

Cheri passed near her once, arms full of wildflowers. Their shoulders brushed; the stranger's hand rose automatically to keep the blossoms from falling.

Tess (softly): "You've woven mercy into every stem."

Cheri: "I—thank you." She blinked. "Do I know you?"
Tess: "Not yet."

Before Cheri could reply, Tess smiled—a small, knowing curve—and slipped back into the crowd. Cheri stood for a moment, frowning at the lingering warmth on her arm, then shook her head and hurried on.

At the food tables, Patty barked instructions like a benevolent general, waving pies into formation. She nearly collided with Tess carrying a kettle.

Patty: "Mercy! You move like smoke. Haven't seen you before."
Tess: "I came with the evening. Thought you might need another pair of hands."
Patty: "If you can ladle soup and argue about measurements, you're hired."

They worked side by side for a while. When the rush ebbed, Tess wiped her hands and spoke quietly.

Tess: "It's beautiful—the way they've turned mourning into music."

Patty: "They needed a day that didn't hurt."

Tess: "Then let it end with promise."

Patty looked at her, curious. "Promise of what?"

Tess's eyes lifted toward the sky, where the first stars blinked awake.

Tess: "Before dawn fades, mercy must bind with dawn—tonight. Waiting tempts the storm."

The words were so calm that Patty almost didn't feel the weight of them until after Tess moved away. When she turned to ask what that meant, the woman was gone—only a faint shimmer where lantern light met mist.

Lanterns on the River

Across the square, Joe laughed at something Leron said, completely unaware of the quiet directive now set in motion.

The river rippled once, though there was no wind.

Night descended as gently as breath over glass. The valley glowed—lanterns in every color swaying from poles and trees, their reflections trembling on the slow, silver water. Music softened to lullabies. The air carried the scent of honey, smoke, and the faint sweetness of crushed petals underfoot.

Joe stood on the riverbank beside Cheri, both of them holding small paper lanterns painted with gold spirals.

Cheri: "When I was little, I used to wish on these. I thought the river carried them to the heart of the world."
Joe: "Maybe it does."
Cheri: "Then make one for yourself, Heart of Dawn. Even miracles deserve wishes."

He smiled, hesitant. "I wouldn't know what to ask for."

Cheri: "Then let mercy decide."

They released their lanterns together. The two lights drifted side by side, merging reflections until it was hard to tell which belonged to whom.

Behind them, the village gathered, singing low— the refrain Janis had written now sung like a prayer.

"Love stays longer than fire,
Light outlives the flame.
Mercy remembers morning,
And calls the dawn by name."

As the last note faded, Patty clapped her hands.

Patty: "Listen to me, all of you! We can't end a day like this with just singing. Every festival needs a blessing to close it!"

Laughter and cheers answered. Someone shouted, "Then give us one!"

Patty turned, searching for the silver-haired stranger who'd been helping earlier—but Tess was already at her side, eyes bright with quiet certainty.

Tess (softly): "End it with a vow of gratitude—two hearts, one promise of mercy."
Patty: "A vow, huh?"

She looked between Joe and Cheri. The crowd followed her gaze, murmurs rippling like wind through tall grass.

Villager: "A wedding!"
Another: "Let the festival end with love!"

Cheri's eyes went wide. "Patty—no—"

Patty (grinning): "The people have spoken, child. Even the winds seem dressed for the occasion."

Joe blinked at her, half-laughing, half-stunned.

Joe: "You're serious?"
Patty: "Never more so. Tomorrow's work can wait; tonight's for blessings."

The crowd cheered again, the chant rising playful but powerful:

"Let mercy stay—let light be bound!
Let mercy stay—let light be bound!"

Let Light Be Bound

Lanterns lifted from every hand, hundreds at once, swirling upward on a soft wind that hadn't existed a moment before. They rose in patterns like constellations, weaving the words into the night.

Cheri looked up, laughter trembling into awe.

Cheri (whispering): "They mean us."
Joe: "Then I guess we'd better find something to wear."

Tess watched from the edge of the crowd, her reflection rippling beneath the bridge. For a moment the light caught her face—pride, sorrow, inevitability. She whispered to the river, though no one heard:

Tess: "Love's hour has come."

The lanterns drifted higher, their glow merging
with the stars until it was impossible to tell where earth
ended and sky began.

Chapter Sixteen – The Unfinished Wedding

'When joy reaches its brightest flame,

the veil between worlds grows thin.

Love must bind before the light breaks—

or lose itself to the wind.''

A Valley Dressed in Light

By the time the sun began its slow descent, the entire valley had become a cathedral of color.

Petals carpeted the ground where fire had once burned; ribbons of dawn-hued silk fluttered between trees, catching the last gold light. Villagers bustled through the square, laughing, arguing, stringing garlands between poles. Every sound, every breath, seemed touched by expectation.

Patty moved among them like a general commanding joy.

Patty: "No, no, the honey cakes after the vows, not before! We're blessing, not bribing!"

Her voice carried above the clamor, equal parts irritation and pride. Joe, sleeves rolled, followed her instructions as best he could, trying to appear calm while half the town asked him how he felt.

Joe: "Nervous."
Villager: "That's a good sign!"
Another: "Means you're awake!"

He grinned, but each word felt distant, as if the air itself had thickened. The light was too beautiful, too still. The kind of peace that felt borrowed.

Cheri worked nearby with Janis, weaving flowers through a white cord that would circle their joined hands during the vows. Her laughter drifted through the noise, soft and clear. Joe kept finding reasons to look her way.

Leron and Dalen arrived carrying an armful of candles and a tangle of half-burned wicks.

Leron: "You'd think a man who once studied sacred geometry could manage a straight line of torches."
Dalen (dryly): "To be fair, sir, they're not burning yet."
Leron: "Optimism. I like that."

He caught Joe's eye and grinned. "Almost time, brother."

Joe: "Almost."

He didn't say out loud that something inside him was humming—low, insistent, like the earth beneath his boots was alive and waiting.

At the far edge of the field, Tess moved quietly among the helpers. Her silver hair caught the sunlight like threads of starlight woven into shadow. She adjusted garlands, whispered reassurances, straightened a nervous child's collar. To most she was simply another kind stranger, but when she passed near Joe, the air changed.

Tess (low): "Remember what you are joining tonight."

Joe (startled): "I thought you were—"

Tess: "Elsewhere? Not yet. There's still a balance to hold."

Before he could reply, she smiled faintly and walked away, blending into the growing twilight as though she'd stepped through it.

Leron frowned, watching the horizon.

Leron: "The sky's shimmering. Heat from the candles, maybe?"

Dalen: "Maybe."

Neither believed it.

Patty clapped her hands, drawing everyone's attention.

Patty: "All right, people—lanterns by the bridge, torches to the path, musicians tune up! The vows start at sunset, and mercy help the man who spills wine on the bride's garland!"

Laughter rolled through the crowd again. The tension thinned, replaced by the easy warmth of anticipation.

The Vows at Sunset

Cheri approached Joe then, carrying the finished cord of flowers. The colors mirrored the sigil on her arm: gold, rose, and faint silver light.

Cheri: "I can't believe they're really doing this."
Joe (softly): "Feels like the world's conspiring for us."
Cheri: "Or warning us."
He reached for her hand.
Joe: "Let's believe it's both."

They stood together, watching the sun slide toward the horizon. Every color in the sky seemed painted just for them—crimson, amber, and soft rose fading into the promise of twilight.

Somewhere behind them, Tess whispered to the wind,

"Before dawn fades, mercy must bind with dawn. Tonight."

The sun reached the rim of the hills and lingered, unwilling to leave.
Every lantern in the square was lit, their flames small suns in glass — hundreds of eyes of mercy watching from every side. The air hummed softly, like a hymn before the first word.

Cheri walked toward the field barefoot, her dress simple white linen threaded with gold. Flowers wound through her hair, petals trembling as though alive. The crowd fell silent as she passed.
Joe waited at the center of the field — the same ground once scorched to ash. Now it was carpeted in new grass and silver-edged blooms. The wound of the world had become its altar.

Leron stood beside a low table of candles. Dalen carried the cord of flowers. Patty sniffled into her handkerchief. Janis and Michael stood arm in arm, their instruments quiet in reverence.

From the far path, Tess stepped into view.

Her silver hair caught the last light of sunset, turning it into a crown she hadn't asked to wear. The murmuring crowd parted without understanding why. She moved to the center with a calm that felt older than time.

Tess: "Let this field remember what fire forgot. Let mercy and dawn bind their halves, and through them, the world."

She lifted two small shapes from the table — the twin sigils she had once given separately to Joe and Cheri. Their surfaces glowed faintly, one with the pulse of warmth, the other cool as moonlight.

Tess: "You each carried a half of the same grace. Tonight, they remember they were never meant to be apart."

She placed one in each of their palms. The symbols vibrated softly, resonant like struck crystal.

Joe's hand trembled. "It's… singing."

Tess: "Because it recognizes you."

She gestured for them to join hands. When their palms met, the two sigils flared and merged — a single rune of gold and rose light spinning into being between them. The glow spread up their wrists, etching into their skin in flowing lines until it formed the Bond of Dawn, shining faintly on both forearms.

The crowd gasped; no one moved. Even the wind seemed to stop.

Cheri felt the energy travel through her, not burning but blossoming — warmth that filled her heart and spilled outward. Joe's old chest scar answered the glow, soft light rising through the fabric of his shirt in the shape of a heart framed in flame.

Tess's voice deepened, resonating with something unseen.

Tess: "You who were once broken by fear, be now made whole by mercy. Speak your vows, and let the world remember love."

Their voices wove together, steady and trembling all at once.

Cheri: "Not to possess, but to protect."
Joe: "Not to rule, but to serve."
Together: "Not to fear, but to love."

The Rift Opens

The light around them intensified, swirling upward like petals caught in wind. The villagers dropped to their knees, faces upturned, tears bright in the lanternlight.

Leron whispered to Dalen, "The land itself is listening."
And it was — the grass bowed, the trees leaned closer, even the air vibrated in harmony.

Tess raised her hands.

Tess: "Then by the mercy that outlives fire, and the dawn that never ends, be bound in grace and remember the song."

The sigil flared once more — brilliant, perfect. Then the sky answered.

A thunderclap split the air.

Everyone flinched. No clouds. No storm. Just raw, shattering sound.
The sunset flickered, and for an instant the horizon fractured into a thousand shifting shards of color.

Tess's eyes widened. "No…"

Wind ripped through the field, scattering petals and flame alike. The merged sigil on Joe and Cheri's arms pulsed violently, resonating with something unseen overhead.

Joe: "What's happening?"
Tess: "The balance—something's pulling it open!"

The air tore with light — not lightning, but a vertical rift, radiant and terrible, opening in the sky above the field like an unhealed wound.

Cheri's cry was lost in the roar.

No other dialogue, rhythm, or imagery has been altered.

Chapter 16 – The Unfinished Wedding

Section 3 – The Rift

The wind came first—wild, directionless, lifting ribbons and flower petals into a spiral that filled the air with color. Candles guttered. Lanterns swung violently, casting frantic circles of light across faces suddenly pale with confusion.

The merged sigil on Joe and Cheri's forearms flared, a golden pulse that throbbed in rhythm with the strange roaring overhead.
Tess turned toward the sky, eyes wide, hair snapping in the gust.

Tess: "Hold the bond steady! Do not fear it—fear feeds it!"

Joe gritted his teeth, clinging to Cheri's hands. "I'm trying—"

And then voices cut through the wind.

Serel: "Enough! Stop this madness!"

The cry carried across the field like a crack of thunder. All heads turned as Serel pushed through the crowd, her cloak whipping behind her like a storm-cloud. Her son, Andaric, trailed close, face twisted in equal parts fear and fascination, while her husband stumbled behind them, torn between protest and obedience.

After the Silence

Serel: "This is blasphemy! Playing with forces you don't understand—this is how fire returns!"

Andaric: "They're summoning it again! Can't you feel it? The air burns!"

Cheri stepped forward, voice trembling. "Mother, please—"

Serel: "You bring ruin everywhere you go! You defy the Temple's order, and now you would—"

The words disintegrated under another surge of wind. The rift above the field widened like a wound taking breath.
Light spilled downward—white, gold, violet—flashing through the garlands, shattering glass and setting shadows writhing.

Leron shouted something lost in the noise. Dalen dropped to his knees, covering his eyes. The villagers screamed and fled toward the trees.

Tess turned sharply, raising both arms as if to hold the air itself together.

Tess: "Stop! The bond's being torn by their fear— Joe, focus!"

Joe's chest glowed again, the heart-shaped mark beating in unison with the storm.

Joe: "Cheri—let go! It's pulling—"
Cheri: "No!"

Their joined hands blazed. The light around them fractured into shards that hung mid-air, spinning. Tess lunged forward, pressing her palms outward as if against invisible glass. A deep, resonant hum vibrated the ground.

Tess (yelling): "Hold the balance! The vow must not break!"

But the rift was already screaming. The sky itself seemed to tear open above them, a vertical seam of blinding fire and shadow. From its edges poured wind that smelled of ozone and stone dust—and voices, whispering, chanting fragments of something older than language.

Cheri's father dropped to his knees. Andaric bolted. Serel's eyes went wide with terror. She stumbled backward, shrieking,

Serel: "See what you've done!"

That cry, sharp and full of faithless fury, hit like a blade through the storm. Tess's expression changed—recognition, horror—and she shouted something no one could hear.

The light inverted.

For a heartbeat, all sound vanished. The world froze in a single flash of white.
Joe turned his head toward Cheri—her eyes wide, hand outstretched—and mouthed her name.

Then the sky swallowed him.

Tess reached for him, her silver hair whipping like a comet's tail, and the light consumed her too.
Both vanished into the wound that split the world.

The rift snapped shut with a sound like all breath leaving the world.

Silence.

Only drifting petals and broken garlands moved in the wind's aftermath. Cheri fell to her knees, clutching her arm—the mark there burned, alive, pulsing in frantic rhythm.

♥ ✳ ♥ ✳ ♥

The Blessing in the Wound

Patty ran to her, shouting her name, but the sound seemed muffled, distant. The glow from the bond faded to a faint shimmer. The earth trembled once, then was still.

The villagers stared at the empty space where Joe and Tess had stood.
Someone whispered, "The Heart of the Dawn is gone."
Another, "The light took him."

Cheri pressed her glowing arm against her chest and whispered through tears:

Cheri: "He's not gone. The mark still sings."

Behind her, Serel turned and fled toward the west, clutching her cloak around her as if the light might chase her.

Andaric ran north into the woods, eyes wild with ambition and confusion.

Her father sank to his knees, staring into the dirt, whispering, "Forgive us."

No one followed them.

Above the ruined field, one lantern still hung in the branches—its small flame unshaken, burning steady against the dark.

The world seemed to exhale and forget how to breathe.

Smoke drifted across the field, soft and ghost-white. The scent of scorched silk and broken blossoms hung heavy. Every color that had once danced here bled into gray.

Cheri knelt in the dirt, her dress torn, her hands glowing faintly where the bond still pulsed beneath her skin. The light was weaker now — a heartbeat that refused to stop even when its other half was gone.

Cheri (hoarse whisper): "He's alive. I feel him."

Patty dropped beside her, skirts muddied, eyes red from wind and smoke.

Patty: "Child… what was that?"
Cheri: "The vow didn't break. I can still hear it — like a song, somewhere far off."

Patty hesitated, then took Cheri's trembling hands. The faint warmth passed between them, enough to ease the shaking.

Patty: "Then we'll keep listening till he finds his way back."

The villagers stood in stunned silence around the ruined altar. Leron and Dalen moved among them, gathering the fallen lanterns, relighting what small flames remained. One by one, people began to kneel, murmuring prayers not taught in any temple. Gratitude and grief mingled on every tongue.

Janis's voice finally broke the stillness.

Janis: "Look."

Where Joe and Tess had stood, the earth had cracked open — not in ruin, but rebirth. From the fissure rose green shoots, already curling into white blossoms that shone faintly with gold veins. The ground itself was healing, sealing over the wound with life.

Patty (awed): "He blessed the soil when he fell."

Cheri touched the new growth; warmth spread up her arm, matching the beat in her mark. She closed her eyes and felt it — the same current that once flowed between her and Joe, now echoing through roots and petals.

Cheri: "He's still healing. Somewhere."

She looked to the horizon, toward the mountains where dawn would rise.

♥ ✳ ♥ ✳ ♥

Where Dawn Points the Way

Cheri: "He always said mercy remembers morning."

Patty stood, wiping her face.

Patty: "Then we'll remember with it. This place stays sacred — a garden for what love began."

Leron nodded. "A shrine to the Heart of the Dawn."

Cheri (quietly): "And to the light that stays."

The villagers began to work again — not to rebuild, but to honor. Broken garlands became wreaths; shards of glass were pressed into soil as glimmering offerings. In the center of the field, a single lantern was set upon a stone, its flame unwavering.

Cheri lingered beside it until night fell. When she finally rose, her hand brushed the air where Joe had

vanished. The mark on her arm pulsed once —
answering, faint but certain.

Cheri (to the dark): "I'll find you, love. Wherever
the light carried you."

The wind stirred, and the lantern's flame bent
eastward — toward the unseen dawn.

Chapter Seventeen – The Circle of Dawn

"When light is scattered, gather the embers.
When faith is silenced, teach the silence to sing."

Embers of the Broken Wedding

Morning crept softly over the valley, painting the ruins in gold and ash. Dew shimmered on every broken garland. The field where the wedding had shattered now breathed with new life — tiny blossoms pushing through cracks in the soil, their petals glowing faintly as if they remembered the ceremony better than anyone else.

Cheri sat beside the single lantern still burning from the night before.
Its flame was weak, yet unyielding — a pulse of light refusing to fade.

Patty arrived first, carrying two cups of tea.

Patty: "You didn't sleep."
Cheri: "I was afraid the light would go out if I did."
Patty: "It won't. Some things stay lit because they've decided to."

They sat in silence while birds began to sing, hesitant at first, then braver with each note.

Leron and Dalen approached from the bridge, faces drawn but steady.
Janis and Michael followed close behind, their instruments slung across their backs, ribbons from the festival still tangled in the strings.

A Circle Forms Around the Flame

Without a word, they formed a circle around the lantern.

Leron broke the silence.

Leron: "I dreamed last night that the fire kept burning because it was waiting for a name."
Cheri: "It has one. He gave it to the world — The Heart of the Dawn."
Janis: "Then this place should bear that name."

They all looked toward the growing garden. The white blossoms had spread overnight into a ring of color, enclosing the center of the field like a living halo.

Patty knelt, tracing the soil.

Patty: "The world is healing through you, child. Through all of us, maybe."

Cheri shook her head. "No. Through him. And I'm going to find him."
The others exchanged glances — none surprised, only solemn.

Leron rested a hand on her shoulder.

Leron: "Then we'll help the world stay alive until you do."

♥ ✳ ♥ ✳ ♥

Teachings for the Healing of the World

Dalen opened his satchel and drew out the small, weathered copy of Joe's journal.

Its edges were newly bound with fresh leather, pages interleaved with careful notes.

Dalen: "There are people who need these words. Villages that lost their healers when the Temple fell. We can teach them what he wrote — how faith mends what fear divides."

Patty: "Then that's what we'll do. We'll carry the song until it finds its singer again."

Cheri looked up. A breeze rippled through the flowers, bending them all in the same direction — east, toward the sunrise.

Cheri (softly): "East. That's where he is."

The others followed her gaze. The sun was climbing, and for the first time since the rift, its warmth felt gentle again.

Patty poured the last of her tea onto the soil beside the lantern.

Patty: "For the light that stays."

One by one, they repeated it — a vow, a prayer, a beginning.

All: "For the light that stays."

The Lantern Points East

And as they stood together, the mark on Cheri's arm glowed once — faint, answering, alive.

By midday the valley had filled with quiet labor. What had been wreckage at dawn was now an altar in bloom: villagers gathering fallen branches to form benches, children collecting shards of colored glass from shattered lanterns and pressing them into the soil to catch the light. The air smelled of new grass and faint smoke—like the world deciding to keep breathing.

Cheri stood at the center, hands clasped before her. The others ringed her: Patty, Leron, Dalen, Janis, Michael, and a few townsfolk who had not fled when the rift split the sky.
The small flame still burned atop the stone.

Cheri: "He wanted to heal the world, not rule it. If he's alive, he's still doing that. And so will we."

Leron nodded.

Leron: "Then it needs a name, so others will know what to follow."

Patty crossed her arms. "We're not a temple, and we're not priests."

Janis: "No. We're witnesses. We saw mercy and dawn touch. That's enough."

Dalen knelt and began to draw in the dirt. His fingers traced a rough circle around the lantern, closing it with a single, deliberate line.

♥ ✳ ♥ ✳ ♥

Founding the Circle

Dalen: "Everything begins and ends in light. Call it what it is—the Circle of Dawn."

The words settled over them like a benediction. Cheri stepped into the circle, the mark on her arm faintly glowing.

Cheri: "Then let it mean this: wherever the light reaches, love will follow. Wherever fear breaks, we will mend it."

Patty removed her apron and tore a strip from its hem, tying it around the lantern's base. "Then it's founded. Not by law. By heart."

Leron laid Joe's spare journal beside the flame.

Leron: "This will be the first teaching we carry. His words will guide others until he can again."

Janis raised her flute, letting one clear note drift over them—a soft, hopeful sound. It lingered, trembling like dawnlight on still water.

Cheri looked east once more.

Cheri: "I'll go where the bond leads. East, to the mountains."

The Light That Stays

Patty touched her shoulder. "Then we'll spread the word north and south. When you find him, you'll find us again."

They joined hands around the lantern, six voices speaking as one.

All: "We are the Circle of Dawn.
We will carry the light that stays."

When they released, the breeze lifted the petals from the ground and scattered them skyward. For an instant, the entire field shimmered—petals catching sunlight like sparks of faith. Then the wind carried them in every direction, as if the world itself were delivering their promise.

Chapter Eighteen – The Voice in the Light

"When all that was divided has fallen silent,
the smallest ember still remembers its song."

When the Lantern Spoke

Night returned gently over the valley, cool and starlit.

The new garden shimmered faintly, each blossom reflecting the pale gleam of the moon. The villagers had gone home hours ago, leaving only the circle—their lantern still burning steady at the center.

Cheri sat alone before it, knees drawn to her chest. Sleep had refused her. The mark on her forearm throbbed softly with its quiet rhythm, neither pain nor peace—just reminder.

Cheri (whispering): "If you can hear me… I kept the promise."

The flame flickered once. Then twice. Then held perfectly still.

A breeze swept across the field, but the air no longer smelled of smoke—it smelled of rain long past, of stone cooled by dawn. The petals trembled, and faint light rippled outward from the lantern as though the world itself had exhaled.

Then a voice rose within the shimmer.
Soft at first, then clear as glass.

Tess: "Do not mourn what was taken by mercy, child of light."

Cheri froze, eyes wide. The lantern's flame elongated, its color turning pale silver. Tess's reflection shimmered in it—translucent, half shadow, half starlight.

Cheri: "Tess?"
Tess: "What remains of me."

Echoes of Tess

The image smiled, tender and sad.

Tess: "I freed him from the rift, but it sealed around me. The void holds its debt. I can send only echoes."

Tears blurred Cheri's vision. "Is he alive?"

Tess: "Yes. The bond still sings through you both. Wherever he walks, the world heals beneath his steps. And you—you must follow the melody east. It will lead you when all paths seem lost."

Cheri pressed a trembling hand to her arm. "How will I find you?"

Tess: "When mercy and dawn reunite, the gate will open. Until then, remember: every act of love lessens the darkness that binds me."

The light flickered, the form beginning to fade.

Cheri: "Wait—please—"
Tess: "Do not wait. Walk."

The flame flared once more—brilliant, blinding— and then steadied, gold once again. The voice was gone.

Cheri knelt there long after the light stilled. When the wind finally returned, she rose, turned east, and whispered to the night:

Cheri: "Then I'll walk."

Dawn Without Trumpets

The lantern's flame leaned eastward, answering her vow.

Dawn broke without fanfare.
No trumpets, no thunder. Only birds and the quiet sigh of wind through the valley, as though creation itself was catching its breath.
Mist hung low over the field, silvering every blade of grass. The lantern's flame still burned at the garden's heart, undiminished.

Cheri stood at its edge, pack slung across her shoulder, her cloak pinned with the sigil's faint pattern now etched into the cloth itself.
Patty, Janis, Michael, Leron, and Dalen gathered

around her. Each bore the same expression—a strange balance of sorrow and peace.

Cheri: "He's alive. Tess said the bond still sings. I'm going to follow it east."

Patty wiped her eyes with the corner of her apron.

Patty: "Then that's where mercy leads. We'll go north and south, take his words to the people who still believe the Temple's ashes mean the end."

Leron stepped forward, pressing Joe's journal into her hands.

Leron: "Keep the original. We'll carry the copies. His voice belongs with you."

Dalen nodded, adjusting the satchel of transcribed pages.

Dalen: "We'll teach what he wrote, what you both lived—how faith and love heal what fear divides."

Janis smiled through tears.

♥ ✳ ♥ ✳ ♥

The Last Gathering

Janis: "And when you find him, tell him the song hasn't stopped—just changed verses."

Cheri embraced each of them in turn. The mark on her arm pulsed gently with every touch, as if recognizing family.

Patty lifted her chin.

Patty: "Then it's time."

They gathered once more around the lantern, their circle unbroken though soon to scatter. Cheri drew a deep breath and spoke the words that had bound them from the start.

Cheri: "We are the Circle of Dawn."
All: "We carry the light that stays."

For a long moment, none moved. The morning sun broke over the ridge, gilding their faces, setting the petals of the garden aglow. The lantern's flame rose taller, stretching toward the light.

Then they turned—each to their path.

Janis and Michael headed south toward the riverlands, their instruments slung like banners of hope.
Leron and Dalen took the northern trail, bound for the ruined temples.
Patty lingered last, her gaze following Cheri.

Patty: "Find him, child. Bring the dawn back to itself."
Cheri smiled through tears. "I will."

She stepped onto the road, the sun spilling ahead like a promise. The bond on her arm glowed softly, steady as heartbeat, leading her toward the horizon.

The Circle Scatters

The others watched until she vanished into light. Then Patty turned back to the garden, whispering the benediction Tess had left them.

Patty: "When all that was divided has fallen silent, the smallest ember still remembers its song."

The wind caught her words and carried them east—
toward the mountains,
toward the unseen,
toward the dawn.

Joe woke beneath an unknown sky, the ache of the world still ringing in his bones. But when he touched the pendant against his heart, warmth blossomed— steady, certain, hers. It didn't matter where he had been thrown or what waited in this strange land. It didn't matter how far she was. Love was a pull stronger than distance, stronger than fear, stronger than the ruin he had fallen through. He lifted his head, breath shaking with the promise he refused to break. *He would*

*find her. No road was too long. No shadow too dark. Nothing
in creation would keep him from her.*

The End

"The dawn that stays is not the end of light, but its
beginning."

If this story moved you, please share

its light —

leave a review on Amazon,

Goodreads, or Fable,

or stay connected for future volumes

and behind-the-scenes insights.

📖 Instagram: @jmbb957

📧 Email: jmbb957@gmail.com

🌐 Facebook Fan Community:

www.facebook.com/groups/josephmoro

Coming Soon: Volume II — Faithheart

Because some ceremonies were never meant to
remain unfinished…

www.ingramcontent.com/pod-product-compliance
Lightning Source LLC
Chambersburg PA
CBHW060539310726
48982CB00009B/1310/J